Alice Falling

William Wall

ALICE FALLING

W. W. Norton & Company
New York • London

Copyright © 2000 by William Wall
First American edition 2000

All rights reserved
Printed in the United States of America

For information about permission to reproduce selections from this book,
write to Permissions, W. W. Norton & Company, Inc.,
500 Fifth Avenue, New York, NY 10110

Manufacturing by Haddon Craftsmen

Library of Congress Cataloging-in-Publication Data

Wall, William, 1955–
Alice falling / William Wall.
p.   cm.
ISBN 0-393-05001-7
1. Married women—Fiction. 2. Friendship—Fiction. 3. Ireland—
Fiction. I. Title.

PR6073.A418 A79 2000
823'.914—dc21   00-055392

W. W. Norton & Company, Inc. 500 Fifth Avenue, New York, N.Y. 10110
www.wwnorton.com

W. W. Norton & Company Ltd., 10 Coptic Street, London WC1A 1PU
1 2 3 4 5 6 7 8 9 0

For Liz

Either the well was very deep, or she fell very slowly, for she had plenty of time as she went down to look about her, and to wonder what was going to happen next. First, she tried to look down and make out what she was coming to, but it was too dark to see anything: then she looked at the sides of the well, and noticed that they were filled with cupboards and bookshelves: here and there she saw maps and pictures hung upon pegs.

Alice's Adventures in Wonderland, Lewis Carroll

There are well-known insects which die in the moment of fecundation. So it is with all joy; life's supreme and richest moment of pleasure is coupled with death.

Either Or, Søren Kierkegaard

The function of sadism is not the same in a free libidinous relationship and in the activities of the SS troops.

Eros and Civilisation, Herbert Marcuse

Chapter One

A grey stain on the ceiling. A fly flits on it. The stain is a map of Ireland. Almost exact. There used to be an ancient truncated map of the world hanging behind the master's desk at school, China and Siberia missing at one side where a fire had clawed it. Centuries ago, it seemed. All the childhoods gone, years gone by in a blur like flashing fields passing a car at night. Who winds the crazy clock? Not God. Dilatory now when the night is black and wind and rain throb against the window, strange creatures dying in the swirl of the wipers: now fleet when the bed is warm and there is mother's hand on her forehead saying, 'There there pet.' *Father Bennis standing behind the master's desk, Gargantua's shadow on the world. Gesturing with the pale tumid fingers. And where is Heaven? Nowhere on this map boys and girls. What's this the catechism says? Heaven is a place or state of grace.* The stain is probably a leak, she thinks, an overflow from a sink upstairs or a toilet bowl. A cracked pipe. Someone else's world showing through in negative on the ceiling, like the images of people caught in the lightwave of

Hiroshima. An indicator that such things have been. There are other people in the world. The fly is walking in Connemara, a secret invasion, the good people of the district sleeping in ignorance as the incubus goes a progress through their villages and towns.

She rolls gently on to her side and looks at the bare shoulder and curly brown head of the boy, hears his steady breathing. John is his name. The memory satisfies her. She remembers saying it during the night. John. John. John. A thin light falls on him from the gap in the curtains, a mixture of a watery dawn and the fading yellow streetlamp. Light steals all the glorious colour of his skin – achromatic hair, translucent eyelashes like the filament legs of insects, his left shoulder, a rind of dark hair extending at the armpit. Her body responds to this wan shape in a way that she cannot explain. She notices the warmth between her legs, a weakness in the muscles of her stomach, a slight quickening of her breath. She wants to put her hand on the defenceless shoulder or on the tight hair. She is overcome by tenderness. Then she thinks that she should allow him to sleep. It is five thirty and she knows he never wakes early because he told her that, a point of honour. He is a philosophy student. Philosophy students make the best lovers, he told her last night, they understand tenderness. The true nature of human relationships, he told her, is that in the good ones people assuage each other's hurt, in the bad ones they open the wounds. Later, bucking above her, aloft on his joy, he said, 'We are the lords of summer, Alice. Though deprived of all hope we are gods still.' It was the triumphant cockcrow. She knew even as he said it that the words were not his own, a borrowed poetry. Good enough still. It thrilled her.

The truth was he was not very good at love. It was his youth that accounted for her pleasure, a suggestion of theft. But what was she stealing from him? And his tenderness, he had been right about that. He was a slow, tender lover. Not like Paddy. Paddy was an in-again-out-again man, as he never tired of telling her. Abrupt in beginnings. Brutal in the end.

You know me, he always said. In-again-out-again-gone-again Flanagan. He had heard the phrase on their honeymoon from a TV salesman who shared their table at an Italian resort. The salesman was referring to his own relationship with a thin blonde who purported to be on honeymoon with him. He meant that he always liked women who didn't expect much from sex. The blonde seemed to expect nothing, was glad of anything that fell her way, cast-offs of conversation, second-hand affection. Paddy adopted the phrase immediately.

Paddy is a bastard.

A car hoots on the street outside. What kind of a bastard blows his horn at five thirty a.m.? She thinks the morning has been violated. The simplicity of daylight abused. She slips out of the bed and goes to the window, aware that she is naked, walking over the threadbare carpet of a student flat, her bare feet sensing the cross-hatching, the skeins that bind the fragile fabric thinned by twenty, thirty years of bare feet. She lifts the curtain as the horn sounds again. It is a Merc, stopped in the narrow streets behind a milk van. The milkman is walking down the concrete path of a house across the way. He is carrying three empties. In the early light she sees the semeny stuff at the end of the empties, his fingers in their mouths. The dawn belongs to lovers, and their early morning odyssey is within his dispensation. God is a milkman, waving empties at pale young men and women elated by their first taste of beauty, going home to cold flats and empty houses. The Merc is evil. That could be Paddy down there, foot-tapping the brake, hand poised on the horn. Blow, Paddy, blow. Wake the lovers in their beds. Wake the old men from their hard-won sleep, the old women tossing in their pain, wake the children to another watery day. This is your world. The lovers will learn that. Sooner or later there will be a man in a suit. A banker. A lawyer. A priest. A planning officer. All good things come to an end, they say. Let's face reality – decent profit, respectability, authority. The hegemony of the club tie. Face up to it. And the lovers, the old men, the women in their dressing gowns put out the empties and take in the new milk, and they are powerless. God the Milkman comes in the night and the only sign is the renewal of day. The man in the Merc rules the world.

Fuck you Paddy the Irishman Englishman Scotsman. Someone will go for you one day.

'What's up?'

The boy is propped on one elbow. The other hand rubs sleep out of his eyes. 'What's the noise?'

She turns her body towards him, conscious of the openness of the act, aware that she has never turned her body consciously on a man before, not of her own volition, without shame or subterfuge. She is aware of her vulnerability, and at once also her potency – it is as if she is glowing in separate parts, small coals of heat at the nipples, the thighs. She is shocked by a feeling of warmth in an earlobe he bit, intensely conscious of it now when he looks at her from the bed.

'Nothing love,' she tells him. 'A stupid bastard in a Merc stuck behind a milkman.'

He is out of bed in an instant. He reaches the curtain and her waist at the same moment, one hand lifting the fabric (there is magic in the web of it), the other drawing her to him, her side against his. 'Look at the stupid ignorant lout,' he says. The horn blows again. The milkman waves the hand that is not holding bottles. One finger stands upright.

'Jesus!' he says. She feels excitement in him. 'John,' she says. 'John.'

He does not look at her.

Now the milkman is turning into the next house and the door of the Merc is opening. A head appears, gleaming like chromium, a fringe of hair, wide protruding ears.

'Get out of the fucking way will you!' he shouts.

'Oh Jesus! It *is* Paddy,' she says. Now she sees the numberplate. It's the new Merc. 98 C. She draws back from the window. John turns to look at her. 'Your husband?' Deliberate, cold.

A long blow on the horn. She nods. He lets the curtain fall. The same narrow shaft of light falls on him.

'Didn't you know?'

'He's supposed to be in London!'

'Will he find out?'

She shakes her head. 'He'll go to the office first. He likes to get in before eight. He'll ring from there.' Did he get in early this morning or late last night? Did he sleep at home? Her place in the bed empty, her clothes missing, her car? Her face is pale suddenly, pale rings around her eyes and there is a slight tremor in her voice.

She looks around for her clothes. Someone (could it be her?) has folded them neatly on the only chair. *Tidy yourself up child.* Her panties are on top, her T-shirt underneath, trousers, jacket. Her socks are folded into each other in her left shoe. She recognises the signs. 'I'm sorry,' she says pointing at them.

She means the neat pile, the organisation, the contrivance. He shakes his head. 'Please,' he says. 'I love you.' He swallows three times. His eyes are big. *Look what you did to the seat? Is that the way you were brought up?* 'No. The clothes,' she says. 'I always do that. I hate it.' She rests her hand lightly on his forearm. 'I remember now. I did it when you were asleep. During the night. I'm sorry.'

He takes her hand from his arm and cradles it in both of his.

'Please. I want you to stay but I know you can't. I love you.'

Paddy is shouting at the milkman. 'Fuck you fucking shit-arse bastard,' he is saying. 'Some people have to fucking work you know. Get your heap of shit out of my fucking way before I call the guards.' He has his cell-phone in his hand. The cold glow of his bald head, dawn turning off it, a shiny football.

Alice says: 'When I married him he was different. None of the boys I knew were like him. He was – interesting. Gentle even.' She did not add: for a while.

John nods solemnly, grateful for the confidence.

She turns her back on him to dress. When she is covered up again she asks if there is another way out. He says he will show her. He is dressed too. No, she says. Stay. Study. He laughs.

'I won't get much done today.' He points at an open book on the Formica desk. 'Not much Kierkegaard.' The room is wallpapered in an embossed floral design that seemed to glow all night, an infinite repetition of twined flowers and leaves as exotic through the haze of desire as a night sky in the tropics. A two-burner gas cooker stands on a Formica press, its ceramic coat dulled by grease. The sink still contains yesterday's mugs and plates. A crooked wooden bookcase contains his intellectual property: philosophy books – Steiner's *After Babel* she remembers from her own college days; a battered copy of T.S. Eliot's *Old Possum's Book of Practical Cats*. She catches herself in the shabby mirror of his wardrobe. Alice in Wonderland, she thinks. Or at least in the rabbit-hole.

She thinks there is always another way out. When the great wheel runs downhill it is only necessary to step sideways. No need for silent comedy, no Keystone Cops tearing across the city, no comedians high-stepping before a runaway. Let the wheel go. There is always another way out. Say a woman decides to poison her husband. She fills the cup carefully, measuring out with so much precision five times the lethal dose. She takes more care than if she were measuring Andrews. He dies in agony stretched out on their bed, his stomach churned to curds, does he think of the last woman he fucked? Say a woman decides to blow a hole in her husband's belly. She directs the gun and pulls the trigger though he has never taught her to shoot because it is a man's game. Now, as he dies slowly, staring at his cooling intestines, he wishes he had taken the time.

They tiptoe down the creaking stairs. He kisses her passionately on the first landing, his tongue pushing brutally against hers, his hands on her ass. He seems to find concealment exciting. When the timed light dies and they are in the darkness of the backside of the house, she feels that he would like to push her against the wall and open her clothes. The urgency is exciting.

The back door opens through a skein of webs and balled insects on to a concrete yard with a clothesline and three dustbins overflowing with ancient detritus, the uninteresting archaeology of the long-graduated. The dominant smell is cats' piss. The yard is surrounded by a blackened concrete wall. Lichen and moss thrive. 'Up and over,' he says. She stands on a dustbin. Her feet scrabble for a purchase. He catches her thighs and heaves up. She is on top of the wall looking down at him. On the far side is a neatly kept garden, two neat flower-beds, a narrow border on each side. A spindle-thin weeping cherry tree in the centre. Another orderly world in which milkmen are milkmen and God is for Sundays.

'Up,' she says. For a moment they are both poised ridiculously on the wall, then he drops down on to the flower-bed and reaches up for her. She falls into his arms.

'Right,' he says. 'We have to go round this side of the house. There's a garage on the other side so there's no way out round there.' The hooting and shouting has stopped. Paddy will be on his way. 'Come on Alice!'

They pass silently round the house and unlatch the low gate. A cat sitting on a wheelie-bin drops down on to silent paws and moves off without looking at them. The milk van has just turned in at the top of the street. They see the milkman's face behind the flat windscreen. He watches them with interest, arms folded on the steering-wheel.

'Goodbye milkman,' she says aloud.

'That's PJ,' he says. 'He's decent.' The milkman waves and laughs. As they walk away they hear the clatter of the bottles, a remote nasal humming, snatches of 'I'll Be There For You'.

They find her car outside the Café Grec.

'Jesus,' he says. 'I can't believe I went into that place. I must have been well on.'

She likes the café. She has been going there since it opened because she believed in its bohemian image. She imagined the scruffy customers were students, writers, artists. Once she saw Tim Bredin in there with a blowsy American woman. She already owned one of his paintings. She used to sit and dally over her meal and watch the others, speculating which one was a poet, which an artist, which a musician. This one had a book in front of him. She wondered what it was until, passing within touching distance of his right hand, on her way to the ladies, she saw that it was a manual of some kind with diagrams and very little text. Then she remembered that someone told her Yeats liked detective stories.

He changed her mind about all of that while they were eating last night. Did she ever notice the prices? No writer could afford to eat there. The place was full of rich kids and businessmen slumming, travelling salesmen and Yuppies with cellphones. The women were all bimbos. He was anxious to show her his superiority. He told her the names of the real student bars. He explained to her that no self-respecting writer would waste money on food. Food was something that filled the gap when *the bag* was acting up, something to absorb the acid generated by too much Smithwicks or Guinness. He pointed out some students standing outside another bar drinking from bottles. 'Posers,' he called them. 'Paying extra so they can pose with bottles instead of glasses. Do you know how much a bottle of Bud is? Or a longneck?'

'I missed all that,' she told him. Growing up in the country. A protected life. Marrying before starting university. She had never had the student life. A home to go to. Money. A car by third year. She craved it. She wished for simplicity, a central purpose, a commitment. *There's no way out child. You're in now and you have to stay in.* 'I wish I needed books or pictures or music,' she said. 'But the truth is I can have anything I want. I don't need anything. I just have to write a cheque. Or else they accept Access or Visa.'

'Did I really come in here? This so-called Greek shitheap? Jesus I must have been pissed.' That was after two bottles of wine. He had kissed her in public, a crazy flamboyant thing to do. It was a small town and he already knew she was married because she had never taken off the ring. She remembered her own delirious surrender, the carelessness. Let him find out, she said. I deserve something too. I deserve to escape sometime. What if somebody tells Paddy? she had said to him, and he replied that he would marry her himself after the divorce. He dragged her into a high, rust-eaten gateway and fumbled her, his fingers desperate, his breath hot in her face. Slow down, she said. Let's go to your flat. She almost said your bed.

He is sitting in the passenger seat now. She runs her hand lightly along his right leg laughing.

'You're full of it,' she says. 'I didn't come down in the last shower of rain you know. You're so full of it.' *I was full of it this time. Full altogether.*

'I just never thought I'd find myself sitting in a red MG.'

'I should have bought a different colour?'

'I better go or your man will be home before you.'

'Thanks.' She looks at his eyes when she says it. 'Thank you John. For all of it.'

'I meant it,' he says. 'What I said.'

'I'll be here again on Saturday night.'

He groans. 'Oh God not more fake Greek food.' She turns the key. 'That's me,' she says. 'Take me or leave me.'

'I'll take you,' he says as he steps out. 'Any time.'

The door slams. She pulls directly out on to the street and has to restrain herself from tipping the horn. The quiet houses of Academy Road beam down at her. The gardens are already warming to the day.

The phone is ringing as she comes through the front door. Paddy calling from the office. Got home early. It was his second time. Why didn't she answer earlier?

Did she detect suspicion? That would be unlike him. Paddy was used to possession. He never suspected the things he owned of having a life of their own. When he fired someone (after appropriate redundancy provisions, of course, and strictly according to the terms of the contract) he never really believed they had a wife and children to go home to, someone with whom to share the news. He never believed in other people's mortgages, tax bills, children at school or university. In casual conversation, because all conversation with Paddy is casual, he would pretend to be aware of the world. At dinner parties, for example, he could discuss the unemployment figures as though they had an existence in reality. He could talk about the cost of living index. Social problems.

He blamed society for the crime and drug culture. Misguided government policies that created slums to clear slums. Card-carrying liberal. That was Paddy. The truth was he had no capacity for faith. He drove between home and the office, home/office and airport, airport and conference. He was a member of a golf club and a yacht club. Nothing else had any presence. He didn't play golf any more because he couldn't win, or because the game was not predatory enough. On the water his boat won everything, a master of the rules, the protest, the right of way, aggressive to the point of being dangerous. And he was a member of a gun club. Shooting suited him. Hennessy the GP and Paddy the businessman – the doctor and the director go out to kill. They come home in the late evening with bagfuls of feathers and fur that turn out on closer inspection to be dead rabbits, dead pheasants. Killing things was an extension of his business drive. Owning a computer software company did that, the personal interest he took in the programming, his obsession with the digital. Reality is an analogue device for him, outdated, wasteful. His belief was in binary codes, the esoteric world of noughts and ones where every choice is simple and every event is a switch that is either on or off. It caused a fracture in space. To believe in people who were hungry or who walked the streets by day, or people who spent their dole on cigarettes, or people who spent all day at one of his keyboards and went home at night to grill a pork chop, people who were members of health clubs because they wanted to make friends: these required of him an act of faith. I believe in beings outside of myself. Things outside of binary codes, tracker bonds, offshore bank accounts. I believe in reality the creator. Reality the word made flesh. Paddy has no capacity for reality.

So now she simply tells him that she had been in the shower. That she couldn't sleep. That the early dawn woke her up. Birds in the garden singing their heads off. This is spring, she says. It's almost summer. The magnolia is in full flower. She hoped there wouldn't be a frost. Frost killed all the magnolia flowers last year remember? The daffodils are everywhere. There are bees nosing in every opening.

By the second sentence she knows he has lost interest. It is his garden. He owned it therefore he could forget about it. He would have missed the hint of joy, of awakening life.

'Missed you,' he says. She remembers the wax magnolia flowers going red-brown and then black, the ground littered with oedemic dead leaves. The stubby stamens, black and hairy, useless on every branch. That was last spring, a late frost. 'When will you be home?'

'Seven thirtyish,' he says. 'Maybe earlier. Dinner for eight.'

'Eight it is,' she says.

'Did you ring about the sail?'

She had forgotten to phone the sailmaker.

'No. I'll phone this morning.'

'Fine. I want it for Sunday.'

'How did London go?'

'Great. Talk to you later.'

The familiar sound of the cellphone going dead.

In the shower she scoops gel into her fingers, milk and water colour, reminding her of his semen. She thinks of John first, a shiver of pleasure: then she thinks of Paddy in his Merc. The shower pelts down. 'The bastard,' she says aloud. 'He's some bastard.'

Chapter Two

They say winter and the small hours for old people. Winter takes them off. But Sheila was a child almost, and although it was midwinter and late in the night, this death was out of season. Snow filled the night, and in the spaces between the streetlights it was the night itself, darkness made tangible. Along Academy Road students coming from the reading rooms were hurrying, books and notes clasped tight, exhilarated by the cold and the magic. The pathways were silent and cars crept by on sibilant tyres. Sounds didn't last in the snow: someone changed gear and the sound died as quickly as a shout in space; someone laughed to a friend and the laughter was swallowed up, dead in an instant; a door closed with finality; a bad cough; a muttered conversation.

She was coming from her parents' house. She had left a cosy house with a cosy fire, Mammy and Daddy and Father Bennis contentedly sipping tea in the kitchen. Younger brothers and sister asleep upstairs. And an articulated lorry pulled out across the road. And when the roof came off it took the top of her head with it.

It was twelve o'clock in the city and the pubs were emptying. People were emerging from their television world to put the cat out, take a breath of air, piss in the garden. They were opening their doors to a different world. Outside snow was falling on the hills, obscuring well-known shapes. The world was changing its orientation, if only for a night. Door was mirror, and when they stepped through the world was not as it seemed. The sills of the red-brick houses were fattening with snow. The roof tiles were losing their definition. Chimneys were heavy with it all over the city. The pale limestone of the cathedral was blending with the night. The quadrangle of the college was Heidelberg. Snow piled ridiculous and tentative on the top knob of the flagstaff.

Elsewhere thousands were dying. The bombing of Hanoi hung in the air of the kitchens after the flickering grey screen. The South African boycott. The North. Nixon's landslide was still falling with a dead sound. The air was full of dead sounds, but in that city they were oblivious. Snow levelled everything in the back gardens. It smoothed the rose-beds and the pathways and it silenced the travellers.

Paddy stood in the tiny garden and felt the snow entering his body, the cold, the cold working in, the bones themselves dying, the joints seizing, blood vessels closing down like early-closing shopkeepers, there being no passing trade in such cold, the heart struggling finally to let go. He tilted his face to the sky and hoped for tears.

There were no tears.

Snow softened on his eyes, his lips, his nose.

Snow burned the skin. It lodged on his hair and in his ears.

He decided to sit down.

Death, he told himself, comes quickly in the cold, and they say it is the best kind, that in the last throes a mysterious warmth spreads through the body, a sense of wellbeing that wipes out all the pain that has gone before. He thought that perhaps he had every reason to die and none to live.

Paddy believed it was love, this irresistible gravity by which he was bound to Sheila. He felt at once that there would never be another, and that she was never meant to be his for ever. Too much of a good thing, he told himself. Too much luck. Reflection in later years will teach him that the duality was thorough-going, that their relationship was founded on it. But then, he saw her death as an unmixed tragedy. He was bereft in the best sense. That this bereavement was founded on his own self-ignorance did not make it any the less intense.

He thought of the first time he saw her. She was standing with a group of girls, all clutching cardboard folders, discussing something of immense importance to them – it could have been politics, religion or make-up. He thought the feeling of superiority he had towards those girls was warmth, that his contempt for their intensity was a benign growth. There was something tentative in him then that made her think that she was not quite a part of the radical sisterhood that would lead most of those girls into law or trade union politics eventually. She stood with one foot angled against her flared jeans, one hand to the side of her head as though cradling a wound. In the other she had a red folder onto which was clipped a range of coloured biros. She was nodding in agreement, her concentration undisturbed by the passing crowd in transit between one lecture and another.

What attracted him to her then? He did not know.

He supposed it was her beauty, but in the past beauty had had a strangely repellent effect on him. The words 'beauty' and 'bitch' seemed to go together. Not in Sheila's case. She wore her beauty like a fragile garment.

'Come out now Paddy,' someone said. He heard the voices, deadened by the snow, coming from the street outside. He heard the sound of drunken laughter, then the sound of someone pissing against a wall. 'Fuck. I needed that. Aah.'

'Come out now Paddy.'

Someone was throwing snowballs at his window. They were standing on the street throwing snowballs at the bedroom where he should be sleeping. Soon they would come through the gate and find him crucified on the snow. Paddy got up. His shame would not allow him to be found. Instead he shaped a snowball with a stone inside and crept to the garden gate. He saw Mick Delany and Nora. Nora carried six bottles of stout, cradling them in her arms. She wore black because she said she was in mourning for the world. She had been in mourning, off and on, for two years. Before that, briefly, she was a member of some weird cult, worshipping God through stones and trees. He had found her once wrapped round a dead elm in the college grounds, moving now and then so that her groin scratched on the rough bark. Crazy Nora, Mick called her. Let's go for a drink with Crazy Nora. It was a kind of daring in itself. What would she be saying now? What would she think of next? Paddy didn't care.

'Watch out,' she shouted, tracking the ghost parabola of the snowball against the night sky. Too late. It caught Delany on the side of the head. The snow was too compacted and the stone had no effect.

'Bugger off,' Paddy shouted.

'Hey Paddy? We thought you were in bed.'

'Leave me alone. Get lost.'

'The little boy doesn't want to play,' Delany said. He carried a hurley in his right hand, tilted downwards at an angle, the weight of a clump of boots laced to the boss. He was standing in the gate, angular and upright at the same time. Hair cropped tight. Delany was a hurler. He had the delicate poise, the suggestion of a dancer. He put the hurley down and prepared to join in a snow battle.

'Sheila's dead,' Paddy shouted. 'Killed.'

They stopped. He heard their rasped breath, the coarse sound of survival. A smoke of stout and cigarettes gathering at their faces. The streetlights shaped ghosts everywhere. A few light soapflakes were falling again, feather and dust.

'Fuck her for dying,' Paddy shouted.

'Poor petteen,' Nora said. She put the stout down carefully in the snow and stepped through the gate. She took Paddy's hands and drew him out to her. She caught him by the waist and hugged him. Even then there was the faint pressure at his thighs. 'Poor petteen,' she said over and over again.

He brought them in. They lit the gas and sat staring at the guttering flames. They talked the broken talk about loss. He told them the details of the phonecall.

The bottles went round, never enough to drown them, but Paddy was drunk on grief. His head was full of her face, her eyes, the silent road, the ticking of the dead engine. Nora sang with her head thrown back and her left hand to her ear. She was only listening to herself, and the hand stopped up the ear so that the words and the tune went round and round inside her head.

'We have no secrets, We tell each other most everything now'

But they all had secrets, that was the meaning of the song.

'They found my name in her address book. That was all. My name and the number of the box out in the hall. They said could I tell them who the family were?'

'She had no fucking tax or insurance.'

'Trust the bastards to stay in the heat of the station on a night like this.'

'I was the only name in the book.'

Hard words spat out. 'Fuck the bastarding pigs anyway.'

Later they put the empty bottles in a cardboard box and the glasses in the sink. 'I'll stay tonight if you like,' she said. He was too desperate to say no.

They lay together in the icy bed and held hands.

'Poor Sheila,' Nora said.

'It was a lorry,' Paddy said.

'She was a crazy driver.'

'She was.'

'I loved her too,' Nora said.

Afterwards, it will seem that this was the moment of lost innocence, that ever after they will be defined by their inability to return here. But the truth is more complex and innocence cannot be lost or found. Those who lose it never had it, never knew what it meant.

Who carved out the roadways that edge along the sides of mountains, cut through deep tunnels, gleaming like silver in the rain? Who threw up the millions of miles of stone walls and ditches? These are the great enterprises.

Sheila was driven west and they all followed, piled into one car, a battered, borrowed Escort, soft on the brakes, soft on suspension. They glided over the shattered roads of West Cork. They came to a tiny churchyard and a priest welcomed them in, they shared in the general benediction. Then six tall men carried the coffin, men with Brylcreemed hair slicked back like James Dean. They shouldered the box and took short stiff strides. A family moved behind, a father in a dark blue suit shiny at the knees and elbows, a mother in a tight black coat, a sister. The brothers were under the coffin.

They lowered the box and said the prayers and filled the grave and Paddy had no goodbyes, no words of comfort. He heard the stony West Cork soil falling on her and his soul was empty.

'Look Daddy, this is a friend of Sheila's from the university.' Sheila's mother leading him inwards into the shadows, out of the brittle winter sunshine. The parlour was full of gleaming furniture. Paddy knew that this room was kept locked, the furniture covered with sheets. But it had been warmed into something close to comfort, a fire living in the huge grate. The intimacy of his knowledge was like a scar, it worried him. He heard her telling him their stories, the credible lies that bind a family, the story of their fall. This is the poker Daddy used. This is the crucifix they had at Grandmother's head when she was laid out. This is the table where they ate the Christmas dinner. Where is her room? He knew there was a loft. There should be a stairs like a ladder leading up to a door with a triangle at the top. He wanted to roam through the house finding pieces of her.

'Is that a fact?'

'What did you say your name was young fellow?'

'Patrick Lynch,' he said.

'She mentioned that name all right,' she said. 'Look Daddy. A friend of Sheila's. Patrick Lynch.'

They shook hands.

'You knew my daughter so.' That explains it. These strangers are friends from the college. Everyone else is accounted for.

'I did. I'm sorry for your trouble.'

'I told her not to go.'

'Of course you did Daddy.'

She made a small desperate gesture with her hands, a kind of sudden folding, the fingers whitened on each other, then open again. She opened and closed them several times.

'Daddy told her there was going to be snow. If he said it once he said it twenty times. But she was mad for the road. Oh she was. We couldn't stop her. Sure, she was only down for the three days and she wanted to go back again.'

'She was mad for the books,' Daddy said.

Paddy nodded. 'She was a great student.'

'I suppose she was,' Daddy said. 'She was going to be a teacher.'

'She would have been a great teacher.'

The gulf of might have been. Silence struck them. They each struggled with it.

Paddy was thinking: she came for me: Paddy is beyond the snowy hills, forty miles down the winding road, his face hidden in the white darkness: Paddy's bed. The thought does not affect him.

'Did you know my daughter well?'

'I did,' Paddy lied. 'We were great friends.'

Her mother's hands seized each other again, a brief flutter, a kind of rictus seen at the edge of consciousness. 'She had communion last Sunday at second mass anyway.'

'Thanks for coming.'

There was a knot of lean men and fat women in the kitchen. The men were drinking from small tumblers of amber liquid. They saluted each other, '*Sláinte*'. They were talking about the weather and the price of cattle. They had the familiar, respectful relationship of men whose cattle and sheep occasionally strayed. The women stood in a circle holding lemonade or sherry. They were talking about how Sheila the poor girl was mad for the road. They looked knowingly at each other and thought of drink. Someone said the smell off the corpse was like a distillery.

Delany was talking hurling with one of the brothers. They understood each other, talked names of full-forwards and half-backs as though they knew them personally. Nora was playing with the younger girl, skipping for her, and chanting as her feet touched the ground, 'Ginger, pepper, sugar, salt . . .' There was a bright smile on her face, a kind of manic glow, and her eyes had an inward look, as though what she saw was a memory rather than reality. The little girl watched in awe.

'She's after doing a hundred and fifty,' she told Paddy.

Paddy saw the dark hair, the dark eyes, the slender hands. His heart hammered in his chest.

'What's your name little girl?' he asked. His voice was such that Nora stopped skipping and looked at him.

'Come here to me,' Delany said. 'Let's split.'

The little girl turned away. Nora said, 'So long Alice.'

The car wound back through the darkening fields. Mick Delany drove and as he drove he sang. Paddy and Nora sat in the back seat. They were curled into each other, Nora's hand resting casually in his. She was asleep. Her breath was whiskey sweet. ('Whiskey dear! A girl your age? Wouldn't you have a drop of wine?')

'I'm going to play for the County,' Delany said suddenly. 'That's my aim in life.'

'What about money? Drink? Women?' Paddy's mind was only half on the conversation. He was also thinking of death.

'Fuck all that stuff,' Delany said. 'That's me anyway.'

'I would have thought it was more the drink.'

'What about yourself?'

Paddy thought for a moment. Flashes of stone wall, gables of houses, solitary trees came and went in the headlights.

'I want to make money.'

Delany laughed. 'Not with English you won't. Oh bejasus you fucking won't with English.' His braying woke Nora.

'What is he laughing at?'

'He says I won't make money out of English.'

'Not unless you're Shakespeare.'

'So,' Delany said, 'what's the secret plan? Why don't you take up hurling? The Mafia'd look after you. That's what'll happen to me when I grow up. I'll get too fat for running around the field and the Mafiaman will come up to me and say, Delany, how about a nice thick job in insurance or the bank? On condition, of course. On condition I'm a County selector and I train the minors. I'll sit on my arse for the rest of my days, pointing out the County medals to customers and reminiscing.'

'You have no soul,' Nora said. 'Paddy has a soul.'

'You're wrong there,' Paddy said. 'Delany has one all right.'

'Christ, if I have it's well hidden.'

'I'm the one with no soul,' Paddy said. 'If I had one I'd sell it. I'd be after selling it already.' He was thinking of the car and the lorry and the desolate night. He was thinking of the house and its people and the child watching Nora skipping. He was thinking that he should feel desolate too and instead there was only this sudden ambition to put money in his purse.

It was April, impossible snow falling again, thick and strong for two hours, falling with darkness. By dawn it would be gone. Lectures were on again after the Easter break. Paddy walked carefully and thought about Sheila's car slicing under an articulated lorry, the car and her blood cooling in that other snow, the red blood melting the white snow. He carried a two-litre bottle of Hirondelle wine. He called at Nora's flat and her flatmate said she was drying her hair. She did not offer to let him in but Nora called from somewhere inside.

'Come in so,' the flatmate said.

Nora came out of the kitchen with her head in a towel. She was wearing a red and white caftan and elephant flares, but the electric line of her mouth belied the casual clothes, the clownishness; and her eyes charged him with the opulence of her beauty. 'Snow,' she said. 'Easter snow.'

'That's it,' Paddy said. 'It's a snow party.'

'There's a book called *The Snow Ball*,' the flatmate said. She was the studious type.

'I got an offer,' Paddy said abruptly. 'A fellow who's setting up a computer shop.'

'Finish your degree,' Nora said.

'You sound like my mother.'

'At least you'll have something to fall back on.' She was leaning her hair towards the elements of a two-bar electric fire and rubbing hard. Droplets sizzled on the elements. The shiny chrome face resonated.

'He's getting an agency. From Xerox or someone.'

'Are you coming back here tonight?' The flatmate's question was directed at Nora but meant for Paddy. The flatmate complained once that she could hear every sound they made in the next room. She could hear the springs creaking she said, and Nora moaning and Paddy telling her things. The detail was so graphic that they stared at her for two minutes. Paddy came round first.

'Did you have to listen?'

'I couldn't not listen. I was trying to go to sleep.'

'Jesus!' Nora said. 'That was like the way the parish priest used to make me go through all the hot petting I did. Amazing.'

Now the flatmate and Paddy stared at her. 'It's all right,' she said. 'He only made me talk about it. I had to confess it, didn't I?' But that night Paddy couldn't come and they had to finish themselves off in complete silence, staring at the ceiling, wondering what it sounded like in the next room.

Nora stopped towelling and looked at Paddy. It was six weeks since they made love. She knew Paddy's heart wasn't in it. Neither was hers but they both like the company, someone warm in the bed, the brief pleasure. He liked to get up early and make tea and toast. He liked to cup her breasts, sometimes to kiss them. At times he could be hard, cruel. Sometimes he hurt her, driving into her in rage. Once he struck her, a closed fist on her shoulder. It left a bruise. But she blamed that on his grief. She knew he still ached inside. She remembered what people said in the cult she had belonged to: treasure anger, they said, turn it to good. Sometimes she wondered whether she should try to marry him. But the core of anger in him frightened her. She thought it would ball itself into bitterness in time, that it would strike out somewhere. Sheila's ghost would always be in their bed, a subtle skein between their seamed skins. And she feared that his anger would find its negative in her. There were times when living was merely coping. To get up in the morning. To attend lectures. To read. Each a tiny worthless struggle. Once, a friend studying psychology told her she was suffering the classic early symptoms of clinical depression. 'Fuck you too,' Nora said. 'Pop psychology. Second-hand Freud and salivating dogs.

What would you know about it!' and never spoke to her again.

Paddy shook his head. 'I have to get an early night. I'm meeting this guy tomorrow.'

The flatmate could not hide her satisfaction. 'Nixon is going to go,' she said. 'It's all over the news. Bob Haldeman quit.'

'Fuck Nixon,' Nora said.

'Is there someone else?' Nora asked. Paddy shook his head.

'That's all right so. 'Cause if there is just tell me. I like you Paddy. I like sleeping with you.' She was dancing very close to him, her stomach pressed to his, her hands clasped in the small of his back. She fitted like an old coat. 'I'd like to sleep with you now.'

'Only we wouldn't sleep,' he joked.

'Not much.'

'I can't Nora. I'm up at seven tomorrow.'

'You're serious about it?'

'I'm quitting. This stuff is all shit. Computers are the real thing. In five years every company will own one. In ten years you won't be able to do without one yourself. There'll be no more money by then. It'll be all computer transactions.'

'I never even saw one,' Nora said. 'It's all science fiction. *2001 A Space Odyssey*.'

'You're too nice for me,' he said. It is as though he had been thinking of something else. She sensed an unspoken argument. 'Why Paddy?' He shook his head against hers. The pattern of his dancing changed, his steps less regular, as though he had only just become conscious of the act.

'Come home,' she whispered. 'I'll mind you tonight.'

Again the tight shake of his head. 'I can't Nora.

Sometimes I just can't.' Someone caught her shoulder, a hard-fingered grasp, like bone against bone.

'Paddy, man.' It was Delany. He beckoned them to the door. 'Come here.' Delany had discovered that there are other things in life besides hurling. 'Jesus lad,' he said. 'This fellow has some pure sweet shit in here. Come on.'

In the back room the music was lower. Someone had a flashlight and was shining it at the walls and ceiling. Paddy recognised the sweet smell. 'Sit down Paddy,' Delany said. A glowing spot went round the room, brightening and dying by turns. It came to Paddy and he breathed in, holding his breath. He passed it to Nora. She sucked deeply, drawing the glow down into her.

In a moment Paddy was happier. He sensed that the room was full of warmth. He felt Nora's lean legs lying alongside his. They appeared, in the half-light of his mind, to be longer, thinner than reality. He had an impression of weakness, Biafran legs. He felt a faint stirring between his thighs. 'Sheila,' he said.

'Oh God,' Nora said. She drew on the joint again and passed it on. 'Poor petteen,' she said. 'I know what you're suffering.' She tapped him on the thigh and thrust her shoulder into his, shuffling it a little, like an animal settling down. Paddy sensed her perfect body like land looming to a seafarer, a shape in the darkness at once beloved and dangerous.

'I'm getting out,' Paddy said.

'We all are,' someone said.

Delany said that the whole thing stinks.

'No negative vibes,' someone said. 'Go with it. Peace. Love.' A snigger.

'Fucking shit,' Paddy said.

'Got to get outta here man,' a stranger said. 'Gotta go to the can.'

'It's a fucking Yank,' someone said. 'Fuck off Yank.'

'Gotta piss on ya if you don't move your legs man,' the Yank said. He was doing an MA on Wilhelm Reich (but why in Ireland?) and learning to write poetry. No one believed in him. The door opened and closed, light lying on them an instant and going out. The man with the flashlight pointed it at a couple spread on the floor, her long flowery skirt in disarray. The man was not moving. The man with the flashlight giggled.

Delany started to sing 'The Boys of Barr Na Sráide'. He was out of tune and slightly flat. The American came back and stood at the door listening. When Delany finished the American clapped. 'Great song man,' he said. 'Dylan could do that. Like "The Patriot Game", you know.'

The door opened again. 'The guards!' a man hissed. It was his party, his house. Paddy didn't recognise him. 'Get out quick!'

Paddy heard heavy hammering at the front door. The man said if they didn't get out he couldn't delay the guards. 'And take all that shit out with you.' People lumbered on to their feet. There was no urgency in their actions. Paddy was first at the door. 'Thanks,' he said. He turned back to where Nora was still sitting. 'Come on!' he said. 'It's a raid.'

She gazed dreamily at him. 'I'm so unhappy,' she said. She did not get up to go.

'Crazy bitch!' Paddy said and slammed the door.

He was not aware as he cleared the garden fence of anyone following him. For a moment he thought of going back, dragging her out. It seemed like too much effort. On the street he slowed to a walk and went round to the front of the house. The lights were on and the curtains were open and he could see a Special Branchman carefully taking names. Nora was fifth in line in an orderly queue. Crazy bitch, he thought again. Stoned out of her mind, she doesn't give a shit. He exulted in it, almost stood on one leg to lean over the garden wall and shout it. Stupid slag!

'Hey Paddy,' Delany said. 'I thought you were quitting?' Paddy had three books under his arm. *The Discarded Image*. *The Practice of Poetry*. *The Romantic Imagination*.

'I'm bringing them back.'

'I'm missing my Early Irish lecture.'

'Big deal.'

'It is if I fucking fail.'

'What happened the other night?'

Delany shrugged. 'We don't know yet.'

'They took your names?'

'I thought you were there all the time. Didn't I call you?' Delany was struggling with a shapeless memory. 'You came with Nora. Where'd you get to?'

'I got the nod from your man. I got out.' Delany shrugged again. 'You were lucky so.'

'You're not telling me something.' Delany was shiftier than usual, staring at the toes of his shoes.

'I'm late for the lecture. Good luck with the new job.'

Finals were near. The grass in the quad was newly cut. Students were drifting still, but drifting now between lectures and reading rooms. The library was empty when he handed back his books. He stood looking at the dark shelves and smelling the dust-and-old-leather smell. Near the back of the philosophy section was a place where he and Sheila had carved their names. They used her penknife, an unusual thing for a girl. Paddy touched the carved names. He touched them lightly, almost a blessing. Did she have the knife in the car with her? She always carried it. He thought that he had no single thing of hers, that she had a horror of leaving evidence. She would clean his flat before she left, checking in drawers for panties, tights, vests. Making a mental list. Toothbrush. Comb. Socks. Night-dress. Notepaper. Once she told him that if you left things behind you lost part of your soul, a spirit breaking up in increments. Everything lost was irredeemable. You could not piece a soul together out of discarded bits and pieces, second-hand clothes and hand-me-downs. And in the end she died in parts. The newspapers said she was killed instantly but Paddy sensed her piecemeal death, a cell at a time, her beautiful head leaching into the night air. Sometimes he saw the snowflakes settling on her hair, the gentle drift that given time would have covered her in a perfect shroud. And a soft snow was falling on the car and the engine was cooling, the headlights shorten-ing down to a yellow circle. The lorry driver groaning in his cab, a piece of the steering wheel in his belly. It was a miracle a priest was first at the scene, they said. He gave them absolution.

She did not need to be absolved.

Except for dying. Paddy could not forgive that. 'Fuck her for dying on me,' he thinks. 'Fuck her.'

Self-pity is a kind of warmth. It spread through him slowly, bringing everything into focus, the world concentric on him. She had died and that was a fault. She had taken herself away, wilful neglect of danger, her fault. 'Fuck her,' he thought.

Afternoon sun slanted across the quad and warmed the seat. At ten to five the theatres disgorged girls and boys. Paddy felt older than them, strangely removed. He felt like a man now and these were children. He saw Nora come out. She was arm in arm with Delany, his lean hurler's stride and the jaunty swing of his shoulders obvious even at that distance. They passed without looking, headed for the back gate. Nora's flat, Paddy thought. That made sense. Delany's place was a dive.

Chapter Three

The brown Cortina. Somewhere between the church and the school the lights stopped. They say most accidents occur to people who have embarked on short journeys. The long-distance driver passes through disaster zones, lights in the corner of the eye, ambulances, kneeling priests. The long-distance car hurtles through the night but for the short journey time has stood still: the child visiting a neighbour is thrown down by a passing truck; the woman passing from home to post-office is struck down, her face broken, her body shattered. Afterwards she needs steel pins in every bone: they glow like cancers in the X-ray. The shorter the journey the greater the danger.

When the lights of the Cortina dropped the narrow ditches and overhanging trees sprang backwards. The road was suddenly vast, one with the stony bogs and dry mountains. The dark brown horse that she saw a mile back had tenure still on the edge of her memory, staring balefully across a five bar gate, filling the shuffling night with his hard body. Her darkness was connected to the darkness of one half of humanity, half the world plunged into despair.

She unclipped the safety belt that she had clipped so carefully five minutes ago, a thing she had delighted in, an actual safety belt. In her father's car there were no such things – no radio, no heater, only one windscreen wiper. Instead there was the permanent smell of dogs, the sour smell of fertiliser bags, a suggestion of damp and fungal growth. She remembered how her father tossed her in, a child landing on the broken springs of the back seat and rolling roly-poly against the far door laughing. Her father's car was always cold, the passenger window rolled almost to the top, but never quite meeting the frame.

The brown Cortina was warm, safe until the lights went out. A lift home.

She fumbled for the door handle, searching where her father's door handle was, missing the point that this was a different world, that things were skewed here. In the brown Cortina.

'Don't be afraid,' he said. 'Don't be afraid at all child. Sure we know where we are.' He meant that even without the light he knew exactly where he was.

'Look at the stars,' he said. She was aware of a hand pointing, a darker object pointing at the windscreen. She saw the white dials of the instrument panel reflected in the glass. She thought those were his stars. Her hand found the window handle and she pulled hard but the door did not open.

'That is Orion up there,' he said. 'That's the easiest wan to pick out. I often look up at that wan.'

When she got into the car at the bus stop he had offered her Silvermints or a gobstopper. She said she would like a gobstopper. He had given it to her from a brown paper bag, her hand fumbling down in the sticky mess, the gobstoppers all melted together from the heat of his pocket. She shifted it into her cheek. 'Yes Father,' she said.

'Oh yes. Orion is a hunter. The Greeks were great wans for naming stars. I did Greek in school myself.'

She sensed him easing out, a shifting of the springs of the seat, a suggestion of bones loosening, his feet coming off the pedals. 'The trees are there, of course. If it wasn't for the trees we'd be able to see all of them. Millions of stars. Do you know what a million is child?'

She nodded.

'A million is a huge number. If you took all the people in Ireland and gave every wan of them a candle and made them all stand on a hill you would have three and a half million candles. But you still wouldn't have wan millionth of the number of stars out there.'

He leaned towards her slightly. She had stopped her scrabbling and now her hands were clasped tightly in each other in her lap.

'A million million million, that's a very big number. How many noughts would there be in that I wonder? But there's still more stars than that. That's God's work, child. We can't understand God's work because our brains are too small. God has an infinite brain. Do you know what infinite means child?'

She nodded, but she lied. She did not know what infinite meant, she simply wanted an end to the darkness. She thought about the picture of the human brain Miss Hearne had in the science room. It was grey and ravined and shapeless. God's brain was bigger anyway. She thought of a planet the size of God's brain, the same shape.

'Infinity means something goes on for ever. It has no end at all at all. Like a circle. You can go round and round a circle but you never come to the end of it, isn't that right? Or it would be like falling off the edge of the world and just falling and falling for ever. Out in space there would be nothing to stop you.'

'Yes Father,' she said.

'That's God's work,' he said. 'It goes on and on for ever and ever *in sæcula sæculorum*. Are you comfortable there?'

'I am Father,' she said.

'Good good. I could turn on the heat now if you like. Sure I will turn it on. We could do with a bit of heat, even on a nice warm spring night like tonight.'

She heard the fan come on and immediately felt a rush of warmth on her feet. She heard the engine humming. She heard his breathing.

'Cosy? I like a nice chat, don't you?'

'Yes Father.'

'About one thing and another.'

'Yes Father.'

'God is merciful of course. That's the whole thing. God's true greatness. He'd want to have infinite mercy with a pack of sinners like us to be looking after, isn't that right? Oh we're a bad crowd right enough. The things we get up to. I hear all of it of course. In the confession box. The priest has to listen to every kind of sin you could think of. But – no matter what happens here God's infinite mercy extends to us all. Not wan thing we do is too bad to get forgiven by God. That's what infinite means. Do you know what,' he said, turning round on the seat so that she knew he was facing her. She stared out at the blank glass. 'Do you know what, why don't I hear your confession here and now? Sure tomorrow is Saturday. It'll save you coming in. We could get it over with here and now.'

She heard her own breathing now, a startling short rasp. She tried to control it, to keep it quiet. When she managed to silence her throat she heard her heart drumming in her chest and wondered suddenly why it was that her own heart was so loud and yet she had never heard anyone else's heart beat. Then she had to breathe again, air crackling out of her chest.

'Go on child,' he said. His voice sounded kind. Why was she frightened? She told herself that she was afraid of confession.

'Go on now, bless me Father for I have sinned . . .'

She swallowed what was left of the gobstopper, an enormous lump that needed repeated swallows to clear downwards. For a time she was aware of it somewhere just below her breastbone. 'Bless me Father for I have sinned it is two weeks since my last confession . . .'

'Go on child.'

She could think of no sins. Desperately she searched her mind for something to say, something decent, common, but likely at the same time. She heard the voice of the teacher who had instructed her for communion listing the sins of childhood: missed prayer times; inattention at mass; ingratitude; insolence; lies; unkindness; disobedience. Somehow they all seemed inadequate. Something else was called for that she could not declare, something that was just outside her experience. She felt its presence like the memory of the horse in the dark field, a physical being in her consciousness. It had no name that she knew.

'I forgot my night prayers.'

'How many times child?' His voice sounded tired.

'Five. Five times.'

'Go on.'

'I cursed at my brother.'

'Was it the Holy Name?'

'No Father.'

'What word was it?'

'The F word Father.'

'Which F word child?'

Her lips stumbled on it, the fricative trapped on her tongue. He urged her on – say the word, this is confession, God will forgive everything.

'Fuck!' The word exploded from her, dropped into his patience, was swallowed and drowned and had no visible effect.

'Go on child.'

'That's all Father.'

Then he reminded her of the terrible sin that was a bad confession. 'We must put everything before Our Lord,' he said. 'All our sins. We have to lay them out for him to see them. Every sin is like a torture for Our Lord. He hates them all. But remember God's infinite mercy. He will forgive anything.' There was a small metal crucifix on the dashboard, dots of purple at the hands and feet, an agonised Christ facing sideways towards the driver. He reached out and closed his fist over the figure for a moment and she saw it was a kind of blinding, hiding God's eyes, closing off the light.

'Think of the worst torture you ever heard of. Something like those Japanese did to the English during the war. Putting rats in cages on their bellies. Well the worst thing the Japanese did wouldn't be wan millionth as bad as the torture Our Lord gets from your sins.'

She shook her head, sensing a mist clearing from it. She was aware now that for some time she had been able to see him in the lights of the dashboard. He seemed enormous, black, filling the whole space on her right, his bulk containing the sound of the engine and the heater fan so that she thought he rumbled slightly and caused a tiny vibration that went outwards to the car and through her and spread out into the bushes and fields.

'Go on child.'

'I can't remember anything else Father. I always take about half an hour to exam my conscience. I'm really slow.'

'Did you have bad thoughts?'

'No Father.' The words thick in her throat.

'Now now. We all have bad thoughts.'

No was the wrong answer.

'I did Father.'

'Ah. Just like myself. Like all of us. You mustn't be ashamed child. We are all human. Even a priest is a human. We all fall sometime. Go on. What were these bad thoughts about?'

She didn't know.

She said she couldn't remember. She knew she had them because after she had them she said an act of contrition straight away. She remembered that it was last week. But she couldn't remember what they were.

'Was it about boys?'

Yes.

'That's natural. We are born sinners you know. All born sinners. The saints even had these thoughts. St Augustine for instance had them. But the saints were heroes fighting against evil. We can't all be heroes but we have our own little fights to be getting on with. Our little struggles. Did you imagine a boy with no clothes?'

No. Not that.

'Ah. Maybe you imagined touching a boy. Someplace. Now there's a load of different kinds of touching child. Kissing for example. If you give a boy a kiss on the cheek, well that might be ordinary enough. Fair enough. Now the next thing is if you kissed him on the mouth. Did you think about kissing him on the mouth?'

'Yes Father. I saw it in the pictures.'

'Now that's only for courting couples. I'm not a dry oul' stick like some of them.' He laughed a short hard laugh. 'Would you be surprised to hear that a lot of priests of my age would say you couldn't have that kind of kissing until you were married? But I'm not like that. If a boy and a girl are serious, and thinking about getting married, a kiss on the mouth is all right. That's my idea anyway. Now the next thing is what kind of a kiss is it? French kissing.' He licked his lips as though tasting a French kiss there, something garlicky and vinous, exotic. 'Did you ever notice in the pictures the way the man puts his tongue into the girl's mouth. They have their mouths open. That's a French kiss. That's going very far. But a girl should be expecting a man to do that. If she was serious and thinking of getting married. Men like it. I'd nearly go so far as to say that girls like it too.'

A distant car crawled along the main road, the lights sweeping overhead and briefly lighting the ash and sycamore. Then she saw the tail lights winking in the gaps, going north towards the town, the road she had just travelled.

'Now of course, once a girl is married there's a load of other kinds of kissing. Did you ever imagine other kinds of kissing child?'

No Father. She was calm now, interested, slightly excited by what he was saying.

'Oh God, I don't know should I or should I not!' He reached out suddenly and grasped her hand, his right hand darting between her legs and dragging out her right hand from the folds of her left. He held it between his, his fondling it and squeezing it by turns. 'I often think girls don't get enough sex education at all at all,' he said earnestly. 'That's what has half the marriages of this country ruined. The church is all wrong there. Ignorance is bad. If young girls knew what they were in for it would be better for the sacrament of marriage. Would you like me to explain it to you?'

She wanted to withdraw her hand, exerted slight pressure, as much as she dared. Her hand did not come back to her.

'I'll explain about other kinds of kissing, will I?'

She nodded, a slight nod. Fear was rising in her again. She was leaning away from him, over against the passenger door. She could feel the buckle of her school-bag pressed against her leg.

'The worst kind. If it was sins we were talking about now. If a girl wasn't married. The worst kind of sin would be kissing a man down here. Kissing his thing. If you weren't married that would be a very serious mortal sin. Boys might ask you to do that and what would you say?'

'No Father,' she said. She was thinking about it. It didn't sound nice. She was thinking of one time she saw her brother pissing into the toilet bowl, spraying the seat with thin yellow water, his thing in his hand fat like a sausage that had burst its jacket at the top.

'That's my girl,' he said. 'That's right. Say no. You wouldn't fall for that one!' He took one hand off hers and slapped the steering wheel hard. 'Say no!'

He put his hand to the dashboard and she heard the hum of the fan go down so that it was almost drowned in the noise of the engine. 'It's getting a bit stuffy in here.'

'It is Father.'

'Are you too warm. Here take off that anorak. No wonder you're too warm.'

His hands caught her at the shoulder and pushed her forward. She felt him drag the anorak back by the collar and down over her arms. 'Slip out of that there.' She was shocked by the violence of the action.

She twisted and turned out of the trap, forgetting suddenly how to get out of a coat, a loss that frightened her. She thought of her father after Sheila's death, struggling to remember how to bless himself and using his left hand instead of his right. She did not know then that he had suffered a minor stroke, that further strokes would take his hand away from him, his eyes dying, his mouth tangling, the fuses going one by one until the house was dark. She felt now as if she were struggling with her father's death, wrestling that determined eminence with her hands pinioned to her side.

But in the end he was only helping her to take her coat off. There was no violence in it, no heroism called for. When the anorak was off she sat back and his arm was still behind her. He was leaning far over, almost sitting on the handbrake, breathing deep and broken. His thigh was fat, bulging in the black material. She could see a faint gleam on the tip of his left shoe, the black leather gleaming. The moon, she thought. It must be up already. It would be a big full moon, the big open face gleaming coldly in the priest's shoe.

'Practice makes perfect,' he said. 'That's a fact.' She could smell Silvermints on his breath.

'You're right to say no until you're married. But when you're married and you have the blessing of the sacrament you could do it. You could kiss it. Because it would be part of the whole thing. Sex between a married couple is a blessing. So you'd be safe enough that way. But the Church is very firm on one thing. Will I tell you child?'

Her left hand was lightly searching the door for the handle again.

'The church is very firm that the sexual act itself is not for pleasure. It's for procreation. Do you know what procreation is child?'

She nodded.

'Procreation means having babies. That's what girls are made for. You're at that age yourself now. You're at the age of puberty as they call it. You probably noticed that yourself. I noticed that you're getting big here.' His hand brushed her chest and then went away. 'That's a sign of it. Womanhood. You'll have noticed other things as well. You maybe had the bleeding?'

She did not answer, petrified, seeing the blood on her legs, a thin dribble of black and pink, a fuzzy stain on the sheets and night-dress, spots of blood like fat stars on the bedroom lino.

'Girls call it the curse, but it's not a curse at all. It's a blessing from God. It means you are getting ready for God's great purpose.' He placed his hand firmly on her stomach. 'You maybe get a bit of pain with it. Here and here. But that's not the worst pain. It's a sign that God has marked you out.'

His hand caressed her stomach a moment as though attempting to assuage her pain, then lifted off and went back into the darkness of his suit.

'It's all for having babies. The chest and the bleeding. And of course, child, the kissing is all part of God's grand design as well. In the heel of the hunt it's not pleasure at all. So if you do it. What I was talking about. Kissing down here. You're not to let him spray into—'

'I have to go Father. My Mammy is expecting me any minute.'

He drew away quickly. 'Sure I'll drive you up. I said I would.'

'I wouldn't mind the walk.'

'Under the stars?' He sighed. 'A walk under the stars.'

The headlights came on silently. She saw a pair of eyes watching them, a startled fox poised in the act of jumping into the ditch. Then the eyes blinked out and she saw a sinuous shape disappearing through a gap in the whitethorn.

He engaged the gears then disengaged again. 'We never finished the confession,' he said. 'You were saying you had bad thoughts.'

'I did Father.'

'Was it about anything I was talking about?'

'It was Father.' Better to get it over with. Say something. *Say something.*

'Tell me child.'

'It was about kissing a boy Father.'

'Any particular boy?'

'You wouldn't know him Father. It was a boy that came down for my sister's funeral. Years ago.'

'Did you think a lot about him?'

'Ever since then Father.'

'I remember your sister's funeral. What was the boy's name?'

'Delany Father. He was a hurler. He played for the County last year. He was on the telly.'

'Delany? Delany? He was corner-forward. A tasty hurler. Mick Delany.'

'That was him.'

'Didn't I hear something about him? Didn't he get into trouble?'

Arrested for possession of the listed drug Cannabis. Given the benefit of the probation act due to his exemplary record on the County team and the fact that he had recently begun to coach the under 16s. She remembered the story in the *Irish Press*. Her mother read it out in full.

'No Father. He was never in trouble.' This was a lie, and in confession. How to confess this.

'That was the boy you had bad thoughts about.'

'It was.'

'What did you think about?'

She hesitated, choosing her word with care. 'I just thought about dancing with him.'

'Do you go to dances child?'

'My mother won't let me.'

'Very wise. You're too young for that kind of thing. There's an awful lot goes on at dances that mothers don't know about. If they knew about them they'd never let their daughters out. Boys always want something. They'll touch you and that.'

'Only dancing father.'

'But when you think about dancing with this Delany boy, you imagine him touching you.'

'No Father.'

'Remember you must not make a bad confession.'

'No Father.'

'You think of him touching you in your private place.'

Shocked. 'No Father.'

'You do. On your bottom. Or up your dress.'

'I do not Father.' She was crying. 'I never think about things like that.'

'He puts his hand up your dress and he gets it inside your knickers. He touches your private parts.'

She covered her ears to stop the words. She saw her father putting his hands over his ears. He found sound painful in the end, as though his own silence was a refuge. Once he heard a car brake on the road outside, the shriek of a worn brakepad, brief, piercing, and he put his hands to his head and closed his eyes. No words.

'He uses his finger.'

'Stop!' she shouted. She felt his arms around her, hugging her. 'Don't cry child, it's all right. God knows us all. Here.' She felt a handkerchief thrust into her face. She took it and wiped her face with it and gave it back. His left arm enclosed her shoulders. His right had the handkerchief.

'It's all out now. God knows the thoughts of your heart. He'll forgive you. I'll give you the absolution now. Will I? Don't cry child. *Absolvo te* . . .' He waved his right hand in front of her face like a good fairy waving a magic wand, except that she did not feel any richer for it. His left hand enclosed her shoulders like an iron hoop.

When the words trailed off he left his hand round her a moment, then he squeezed her left shoulder and removed his hand. He engaged the gear and let the clutch out. The car moved off gently, the lights brightening as the engine revved. 'There now,' he said, 'you got that off your chest. You'll feel better after that.'

He began to hum a tune. He moved his hands very little as he steered. They were almost joined across the top of the wheel. He directed their path through the darkness with minute adjustments, humming.

'We'll have another little talk another night,' he said after a time. 'Your daddy asked me to look after you before he passed away, did I ever tell you that? That night I brought him extreme unction. It was like God gave him the gift of speech wan last time. He was able to make a good confession the poor man. And says he to me, says he, "Look after Alice Father". I promised him. I said I would. So we'll have another talk another day.'

The lights swept the front of the house. The curtains glowed in her mother's room. The kitchen was in darkness.

'Your mother won't be worried because I was in earlier. That's when she told me you were coming on the bus. Now that you're in secondary you'll be home late every Friday, isn't that it? That's what your mammy said, because of the gym. Do you like gym?'

She nodded.

'I often watch the gymnastics on the telly. I love it. Do you do gymnastics?'

'I'm only starting.'

'Still. *Mens sana in corporo sano*. You're not doing Latin? A healthy mind in a healthy body. That's a good saying. Your mother won't be worried because I said I'd collect you off the bus. She won't be worried at all at all.'

'I better go Father.'

'Remember everything you told me is a secret. The secrets of the confessional. Don't be afraid that I'll ever say a word of it to anyone. I'll take my secrets to the grave. We all have our secrets that we can't tell anyone. And don't be ashamed either child. We all have bad thoughts at times. Because we're all human. You can make a good confession to me. Say a prayer for me tonight child.'

'Yes Father.'

'The handle is there.' He leaned across her, the weight of his shoulders crushing her small right breast. She could smell the must of his black coat, the smell of closed up rooms and old dry women. The smell of sweat, hair oil, Silvermints.

The door opened.

When she was caught in the headlights, a spindly girl in a dark blue pinafore uniform, legs unnaturally white, he rolled down his window and called 'Alice'. She did not turn even when he called her name a second time and louder. She walked steadily towards the house, her school bag in one hand. When the door closed and the light came on in the kitchen he shrugged and carefully folded her anorak, inside out, on his lap. He left it there to warm his belly as he drove away.

Chapter Four

'Galleria Clary invites you,' she says. Paddy glares at her. He picks up a piece of bread and shoves it into his mouth. A crumb falls from his lips and tumbles to the floor. She has to resist the temptation to pick it up. Light streams on to the high polish of the table, the marquetry of the rim gleaming in geometric shapes. Was it weeks since she had slept with the boy? He had the same way of forcing food into his mouth, the Café Grec's best imitation of garlic bread. She remembered the garlic on his breath, sweet taste of darkness and skin.

'I'm watching this Federal action closely,' he says, tapping the paper. 'I'm into the States too much. If Intel loses it could mean a shake-up. I'll be there in my own small way.' Intel and the Feds locked in mortal combat over God-knows-what esoteric piece of numerology. Intellectual property, probably. She yawns quietly and then straightens her face. He does not notice the yawn. He continues jabbing the article with his index finger from time to time.

'It's Tim Bredin. Work he did when he went west.

Clare and Galway. You'll like it.' She longs for the grey cold of the West, the pure air. Not home. Someplace anonymous in the full face of the Atlantic, the simplicity of stone and sea.

'No more fucking pictures,' he says. 'The house is full of them.'

'You're a patron of the arts,' she says. 'A man of substance.'

'That poofter Cleary!' He looks up and then covers his mouth with a coffee cup.

'Oh no, not that again.'

'Not what again? He is a poofter or whatever he wants to call himself. He doesn't make a secret of it. Did you ever feel the way he shakes hands?'

'He always kisses me.' The picture comes to her of the boy's kiss, his face above hers. She shivers and shakes her head to cover it. It is three weeks since that night. She has managed to encapsulate it, keep it isolated from the rest of her life. Better to be safe than sorry. But she has always been good at such separations. *Our little secret, child. Yes Father.* It was a good training.

'No danger there.' He is talking about Billy Cleary.

'Paddy!'

'What? Look I think I'll be busy.'

'I checked. You won't.'

He picks up a pen and toys with it. It is a brief interlude. The pen whirls in his fingers once, twice, two full somersaults, then he slaps it down and folds his hands on the table.

'I suppose you said I was going?'

'I did.'

'Jesus Christ almighty.'

He folds the newspaper and puts it to one side. In the bottom right-hand corner is an article headed: 'Wife Remanded for Double Murder'. Now there are papers beside his plate, the gaping maw of his briefcase on the next chair. She can see the headed sheets: Micro Solutions. It is his software company, the one that creates tailor-made software for particular businesses, his pride and joy, his first venture on his own. In the early days he had simply offered to design programmes in D-Base, a commercially available system, to keep track of stock. His other speciality was CPM, an early operating system. When DOS came on the scene he had almost died. It took her urging to show him that what IBM wanted would become the future. He made the conversion just in time. Now when the Federal Trade Commission sues Intel he thinks it may hurt him or help him, depending on the shake-up. Every disaster is an opportunity for Paddy. One of his other interests. Still, Micro Solutions, the smallest component in his portfolio, is his first love.

'Your friend called.' She can hear the thin voice on the other end of the line even now. 'Is Paddy there?' No he is not here. 'I'll try his mobile.' Do.

'Who are we talking about?' He feigns nonchalance. She wonders, not for the first time, if there is some truth in her innuendo.

'That bloody lunatic woman. Nora.' She isn't sure about that. It is no more than a guess. So many people call for Paddy, and so many women. It was because he couldn't leave the office behind. His drive is endless. She doesn't really suppose he would take the time to have an affair.

Paddy gets up and opens the door. 'She's not a lunatic. Anyway, what did she want?'

In a moment he will leave. She sees that his coffee cup is angled crazily on the saucer, his knife is tilted blade up, marmalade sliding down on to the tablecloth. She wants to reach out to put things right but knows that it will have to wait until he is gone.

'Your problem is you can't credit me with doing anything decent. You think I'm completely mercenary.

That's your problem. I'll phone if I'm going to be late.'
And he is gone. She hears the mewing of the Mercedes
engine and knows by the change of light in the windows
that his car is backing out into the sunlight. *The trouble is
you think I'm only using you,* he used to say. *You don't believe
I have your own good at heart.*

A dry gale is blowing up the street when John arrives at
the Galleria Clary. The frontage is plain, like a huxter
shop, suggesting jars of bullseyes and liquorice twists
instead of art. Inside the gallery is really a wide corridor,
angled halfway back at about thirty degrees and sloping
downwards slightly as though headed for cover. The
walls are roughcast, painted white. Spotlights dangle on
steel wire eight feet above the floor. Alice is standing in
front of a pretentious landscape-with-sheep piece.

Look at the way she holds the glass. Her fingers pose
the stem as if she is carefully tilting a fine instrument at
the air, a sampler of some kind, testing the delicacy of the
atmosphere. The wine is a kind of pale amber, very pale.
Her wrist. She is wearing a linen jacket. Even from here,
at this angle, he can tell that she has small breasts. Small
but apple-sweet, perfect in shape and texture. It is not
necessary even to have seen them. Her dark hair.

That's Bredin. Look at the poser's hands. They
divide the air, loop and flip. He believes that artists have
expressive hands. His fingers are like baby parsnips, pale
and tumescent. His wrists extend for almost a foot from
the sleeve of his jacket. He has a small ass and so have all
the women in his pictures. The ultimate egoism. Or is it
some kind of subtle comment (Art my Ass?). They may
have enormous breasts, huge mouths, eyes like saucers,
mountains of hair, but they will have a constipated small
ass. That's a Bredin, people will say. I know it by the ass.
It's a trademark. You can always tell a Bredin. There is

something constipated about the landscapes too. True to the exhibition title, they are soulless.

That must be Paddy. Chromium bald head. Trim with a slight paunch. His hand looks as if it is waiting for a chequebook. His function is payment. Hers is purchase. She weighs the advantage to her soul of owning a small-arsed painting. He is estimating the cost. Give him his due, he probably doesn't think of it as an investment. He will do anything for her. He can afford to.

Bredin has taken her by the waist and is guiding her to the next picture. Fucking bastard. His hand. The next is a landscape-with-cat. The cat half sits on a dry-stone wall, glaring bleakly at the artist's brush. A model cat. Bredin must paint from photographs because that cat is too good. It is the only decent thing in the room, a photo-realist cat in a fake landscape in a fake frame in a room full of fakes in a fake gallery.

Sandy Muldoon catches his elbow. Her hand is proprietorial too. 'So what do you think?'

He has to be nice to Sandy Muldoon. She got him in. She is starry-eyed about art. She works at the gallery for special nights, openings, readings. She is skilled at this kind of thing, whatever it is. She told him when she gave him the invitation that she had high hopes she would be taken on on a more permanent basis. Sandy is the hurt kind, he thinks. Somewhere deep in her past is a shocking betrayal. She hunts constantly for someone who will make it all right, someone who will restore her faith in humanity. Her eyes say it, they search faces, never still. And there is something threatening there too. John is half-frightened of her and half-patronising.

'The wine is all right,' he says. She looks crestfallen. 'Oh Johnny,' she says. 'Is that all you can say?'

He relents, happy to have scored one point. He

wonders at this instinct of his, to wound the wounded, to take advantage of small advantages.

'I think his work is very interesting Sandy. I really do. I'm only acting the bastard. And thanks for getting me the ticket.'

'It's not a fucking ticket,' she says, suddenly angry. 'It's a fucking invitation!' He is thinking: It's funny how so many women become available when you have lost your freedom. I could walk Sandy home tonight. It is as if she senses the boundary, the out-of-boundary that is all around me. She thinks I have given myself to someone else (that is the way people like Sandy think), that I have lost my soul to someone. Sandy wants someone to lose his soul to her. Only in absolute possession will she feel secure. He remembers the first time they met: a lifeless party at someone's bedsit. Eight or ten people sitting or standing. Too little drink. They spent an hour or so in desultory conversation, danced when the music was put on, kissed and parted. Even then she was determined to get out once her degree was finished, and he was hoping to retain his scholarship right up to his master's, a feat that would require a double first. When he got it she congratulated him. 'I don't know how you stick it,' she said, and he replied that he only felt alive when he was reading. They were friends. There would never be more.

'I'm only acting the bastard,' he says.

A fat woman swoops by with more wine. The heat is intense. All those tiny spotlights – that such small lights should generate so much heat! The wine is warm too. 'I'll introduce you,' she says. She puts her hand on his left elbow again and turns him gently towards Tim Bredin. The crowd has filled in a little. He must edge between Paddy and a man in a blue pinstripe suit. They are talking about insurance. 'I need about three million on that one Mick,' Paddy is saying. 'Give me a quote. A ballpark figure. Don't fuck about.' The other man is

pale, intense, nodding his head repeatedly. He says
something about 'Head office'.

Alice is standing so close to Bredin that he must be
able to feel the heat of her body. Heat emanates from
her, a kind of dry heat. Tim Bredin is gazing up at her, a
smallish man with the dark head and mouth of a
Kerryman. When she sees John her eyes register alarm,
then anger. It is as though she has arched her back or
extended claws. He feels the hostility and feeds on it.

'Tim,' Sandy says. 'I'd like you to meet an admirer of
yours.'

His toad-eyes swivel electronically. 'An admirer no
less,' he says. He is disappointed to see it is a man. They
shake hands but John watches Alice. Because he is caught
in the covetous grasp of Tim Bredin's right hand, he is
unable to delay her. She hardly looks at him and the fixed
smile is only slowly fading. It all looks very natural: the
rich patron is taking the arrival of a new admirer as an
opportunity to slip away, to find more interesting
company. She will circulate, sip wine. He feels the lurch
of loss, tipping him into giddiness, irresponsibility. He
thinks that there is no more than a sentence, a phrase, a
verb, between possessing and losing her. Sweat appears
along the line of his eyebrows. He feels the beadlets
there, each individual and separate like blisters.

'And who is your friend?' he asks, desperate to detain
her.

Bredin turns. 'Alice Lynch,' he says, his face regis-
tering surprise as she moves into the room. 'That's her
there. She's a . . . a buyer.' The mercenary term slips out,
ejects itself into the room, brassy like the cartridge of a
silenced gun. His voice trails off and his eyes narrow. He
is seeing lost opportunity. He is seeing a buyer drift back
into the crowd. Perhaps five people in this room will
open their chequebooks tonight. Five red spots will go
up. Tomorrow when ordinary mortals get to see the

pictures they will feel that Tim Bredin is still selling well. Four red spots now. One on the cat. Alice Lynch has slipped away. They are both temporarily bereft, the lover and the artist.

'I like your work,' John says. The landscape-with-sheep is actually called *Soul Meat II*. 'It has a certain existential quality. A kind of in-between-ness that I like. It's really something undefined on the edge of becoming. A thing about to realise itself. I like that.' This is pure bullshit and he is enjoying it. 'The indeterminate edges, the vague, almost opaque quality of the light, as though dawn is just around the corner. The milky white sky. And then the photo-realist touches. The masculine strength of the landscape. I love the hard-edged forms of those fields. There's something very Western-Isle about it. Primitive, you know what I mean?'

Tim Bredin glows. His eyes have gone to his own picture and he is searching for John's words in it. 'You're not a critic are you?' he asks hopefully.

'Sorry,' John says. 'I'm a philosophy student. Doesn't it show?'

The transition from joy to indifference is almost instantaneous. Bredin's eyes catch John's for a nanosecond then filter slowly to the left.

'Excuse me a minute,' he says. 'I have to say hello to someone.' He goes rapidly through the crowd, right arm extended pre-empting a handshake, body tilted so that it looks like he is carrying a rapier, about to make a daring pass with it.

'You're a right bastard,' Sandy says. 'What did you want the invite for anyway, if you're going to do something like that. You were taking the piss. You don't know the first thing about art.'

'Can't help it, Sandy,' he says. 'I'm drawn to crap like a bluebottle.'

A light comes on behind her eyes. He sees not anger

but contempt and it strikes him suddenly that Sandy Muldoon is capable of great loathing. He remembers seeing that once before. She was dancing with someone at one of the college discos, a slow dance. He was feeling her up and she stood back and vomited on him. It seemed impossibly calculated, a wilful projectile of bile. Afterwards people asked her that. Can you just do that? someone asked. Like, just vomit on someone? Yes, she said. I have complete control over my body. People were more careful with her afterwards.

But this is art, the Galleria Clary. A public gesture is hardly called for.

'You're a fucked up bastard,' she says. 'That's the last time I'm getting anything for you.'

She snatches the glass of wine from his hand. 'And no more free wine.' She brushes past and heads for the desk where Billy Cleary is barely coping with the attention of someone who doesn't want to buy a certain picture but wants to borrow it for a week or two just in case his wife does. Sandy intervenes. He watches her sweep the man up and shoo him back into the crowd. Her simple intervention gets the circulation going again and suddenly the whole mass is clockworking around one notch, everyone looking at the next picture. Sandy is magnificent. Now he sees the skill in it.

Money is everywhere. He is the only student present, that is certain. That tall man with the hook nose is a barrister. He has seen him going into court wearing a ratty gown and a grey wig. He carries a big square case. The man beside him is a doctor. He heard someone call him 'Doctor Hennessy'. A medical doctor? Or a doctor of letters? There is more money in medicine. Letters are cheap. Alice fits here. This is her world.

'You're following me.' The voice has a slight tremor in it. He doesn't have to turn around to know who it is.

'Alice,' he says. Billy Cleary passes by with a woman

whose hair is blue-rinsed to a purple colour. The effect is startling. She holds Billy's arm with one hand and an aluminium walking stick with the other. She is bent forward from just below the waist and has to rock back on her feet to see up as far as the pictures. She wears a huge string of pearls that swings out vertically from her neck and looks like it is a counterweight for when she looks up. Beside Billy Cleary's impeccable white suit and gold and red bow-tie, she looks like cheap imitation of gross wealth.

'I don't want people to see,' Alice whispers.

He can smell her now, not perfume because he's not good at perfume, but a less definable bodysmell, a unique signature, a fingerprint in air. 'I'm not following you,' he says. 'I wangled an invitation to this because I thought you'd be here. I knew you were interested in Bredin.'

'I'm not,' she says, surprising him. 'I hate his work.'

'But you're going to buy it.'

'It's expected. Didn't you know? Paddy and I are patrons of the arts. When you have money you're expected to spend it.'

'That's what it's for.'

'Wrong again. Money is for power. Spend it or keep it, it makes no difference. Money is control. It is more of everything up to the point where more is crude. After that it is less but better. I could buy ten other pictures for the price of one Bredin. I've reached the less-but-better stage. I drive an MG, not a Porsche.'

'Is that a statement of some kind?'

'I'm bored.'

'I've been eating my heart out at that Café Grec.'

'I couldn't get there.'

'Just like that?'

'What do you want? I couldn't get away. We had something every weekend.'

'Crap.'

'He *plans* my life. Do you see that?' She points at a formalised seascape with an incongruous and photo-graphically detailed Galway hooker under a blot of red sail, plunging through waves. 'That pretentious piece of shit is what he wants. It's all pretentious, but I know Bredin painted that because Paddy would be here. He knows Paddy likes boats. I'll end up buying that. It looks like a cheap imitation of a postcard.'

'Why not say no?'

The look she gives him makes him feel like an errant child. 'Paddy,' she says, 'is not like that. His whole thing is that people never say no to him. When they have done, in the past, his revenge has been devastating. I could name companies that have closed. On a personal basis, people tend to be nice to him. He has a temper.'

'You mean he's a brute.'

'He can hurt.'

John catches his breath, almost a gasp. 'You're talking from experience aren't you? He hits you.' He could not imagine this beautiful capable woman submitting to a beating.

'No,' she says. 'We have an arrangement. He's a careful man.' But she looks away, her eyes flitting from picture to picture, avoiding his.

'Leave him.'

Her laughter is like glass breaking.

'What?' John smiles down on her. He feels superior and fatuous at the same time, out of his depth and deeper than anyone else in the room, a crazy heady impetus that is driving now towards commitment. He wants to say: I love you, leave him and marry me. He wants to take her out into the night and walk away from everything.

She looks at him coolly, a suggestion of a smile on her lips. 'After one night. That's all it was, you know. One night. There are plenty of one nights.'

She looks him frankly in the eye and she has the fixed smile again. His mood evaporates and is replaced by an equal measure of hurt and anger. 'Fuck you,' he tells her.

'I'm leaving.'

Instantaneous. The moment is past. No time to estimate what he has lost. 'Wait. I didn't mean it—' She is already gone, in fact. She slips through the crowd and he sees her twine her hand into Paddy's arm. They talk. She laughs. Paddy's group includes the doctor and the pinstriped man. No women except Alice. They all hold their wineglasses like heavy weights hefted in the palm. One of them sneezes suddenly and pulls a handkerchief from his top pocket. The doctor says something. Everyone laughs. Billy Cleary hovers at the fringe trying to see whether their wineglasses are full or not. In a moment he makes a dramatic gesture to the fat woman and she emerges from the shadows with a tray of fresh glasses.

Sandy is watching him. How much has she seen?

Alice and Paddy kiss. It is a brief kiss. Two leaning branches touching in a breeze. Alice is going through the glass door. Paddy has resumed his conversation with the pinstripe suit. The same man sneezes again but this time the doctor steps back a little and studies a painting. A woman in a tight black dress edges up to him. They nod together, the woman gesturing at the wall with purple fingernails. She has a wart on one finger.

The Café Grec. That night he waited an hour before ordering, still hoping she would come, that he had not misjudged her. The waiters were on the point of throwing him out. He had moussaka, tasteless, odourless and shapeless. He hated it. (The Café Grec's one throw at living up to its name. Next time, he told himself, it'll be spaghetti bolognese.) He felt like brushing the plate away from him, outwards at the other diners – the inane Yuppies, businesswomen – spoiling the white tablecloth, the mellow pine floor, dousing the candles with moussaka. He did not. Instead he progressed to ice cream and coffee. The cheapest thing he could buy. She never came. Every time the door opened he swivelled ninety degrees to find another strange woman or man. Their plump rugby-shoulders or hockey-knees were nauseating. He expected them to stand shoulder to shoulder and dance to the fake Greek music.

I could be at my desk, he kept thinking. Kierkegaard. Husserl. Existentialism and phenomenology. Another hundred or thousand words missed. The pressure to perform was intense, to justify the scholarship. He thought of the bright energy he found when a new phrase or idea struck him, the burning joy. Then he understood why the myth of Archimedes running from his bath had persisted so long. There were times he would have done it himself, when he felt joined in a small way to the great line of people who had found beauty in thought. And then he thought of Alice and the density of the image was so great he could have reached out and touched it: her breasts with the tiny red-brown aureole of the nipple, the shallow curve and the parabola below; her sloe-eyes and the dark rings that surround them; her hair a rich black glaze.

By the time they were closing the doors he hated her. He imagined things he would say if he ever met her again, hurtful things. He polished the phrases like glass ornaments, rubbing his fingerprint off them, universalising them. Now that he has had a chance to consider it he understands that he was poisoned by sexual frustration, his body driving onwards like an animal in rut, but without the object of the drive. That's all it was. She was not there although his hormones hadn't grasped the fact.

Expecting her for seven days, they were not prepared to be disappointed. He felt poisoned by desire, brimful of wasted waiting. He went home about one o'clock and lay on the empty bed.

Alice is waiting fifty yards away. She has the keys to the Merc. She leans against it, her legs slightly splayed, her left elbow in the palm of her right hand, her left hand holding the keys is pressed against her cheek. When she takes it down there is the faint imprint, a jagged edge on her pale skin.

'I was hoping you'd follow me out.'

He wants to catch her but she twists out of his grasp and goes around the front of the car. 'Get in will you.'

She drives slowly. There is a Beethoven concerto on the CD. The cello moans around the enclosed cabin. The dull light of the instruments.

'I missed you,' she says.

What will he say? That he has managed somehow, despite the bad food in the Café Grec. That he lost himself in his work. That Husserl is fascinating. That the phenomenon is paramount. That their lives are no more than isolated particles, each experienced singly, but looped together like an infinite necklace by the unconscious. That these brief moments that they have shared are nothing by comparison with the vast loneliness of the in-betweens.

She stops at a woodland lay-by. Before she kills the lights he is aware of a pine picnic table, a rubbish bin, grass, and the dark insistence of the trees. She does not look at him. She stares half-sideways, as though studying something in the wing-mirror. Involuntarily he looks over his shoulder but there is no admonitory figure coming from the road.

'Do you want me or not?'

He looks down at her long legs. 'I do.'

'So don't waste time,' she says.

'Paddy will kill me if he finds out.'

'That you're having it off with me.'

She giggles like a schoolgirl. 'That's a crude way of putting it.'

'Having an affair with a philosophy student so.'

'No. He loves this Merc. If there's a semen stain on the seat he'll murder me.'

'Will he know it's semen?'

She shakes her head. 'I'll tell him it's ice cream.' They chuckle.

The engine is purring, almost silent. There is no vibration. 'I'm going to kill him instead,' she says. 'I hate him.'

'Why don't you come to a party with me. Only students. No one would know who you were. We're all poor.'

'Someone would be bound to know.'

'Not my friends. Nobody knows anybody.'

She pulls out on to the road. In the distance a pair of lights winks between trees. 'All right. I'm going to be free next weekend.'

'Saturday night so. Don't bring the MG. Walk. Meet me at my flat.'

'You're sweet,' she says.

He does not say he loves her, although he thinks he does. He has grown up since their first night. He has glimpsed the interior from her standpoint, a different world, a separate code. Connections there are chilled, brittle. The leaning branches kiss, the pinstriped suit, the careful laughter, needing three million on that, don't fuck about. He does not have the key to how she lives. He hopes if he can be near her long enough he will find it.

They drive back through the streets. The pubs are emptying. They pass the gallery and Sandy Muldoon is outside talking to the owner and someone else. She does not see the Merc glide by. 'What about Paddy?' he asks. She shrugs.

'I know nothing about you really,' he says. 'Even though we spent a night together. For instance, where did you come from? Have you any family besides Paddy?'

She shrugs again.

'Why don't you have children?'

'I came from the country,' she says. 'I married Paddy. I don't want children and Paddy couldn't care less.'

'Why?'

'Look,' she says. 'You fucked me twice. It doesn't give you the right to investigate me.'

'It does.'

'I had an unhappy childhood. All right. Does that satisfy you? I hate children. Besides, I don't exactly want to perpetuate Paddy's image.'

'OK,' he says quietly. 'I get the picture.'

She thinks he is sulking. For a moment she stares at the windscreen. Then she breathes sharply through her teeth and turns towards him. 'Just don't ask me about that,' she says. He holds up his hands in a gesture of surrender. 'My fault,' he says. 'Sorry.'

'No. Some people think talking helps. Softens things. I don't. Silence is better. Words open wounds.' Suddenly she finds herself choked by the need to confess. Her mouth forms the word but no sound comes. She swallows once, twice. Jesus, she thinks, what's happening to me? This boy's softness unnerved her: years of silence, coping, suppressing, nights and days of studied coldness, and a few hours of simple love unbinding everything.

'A burden shared . . .' he says.

'No! You know nothing about me and you never will.

Forget it. I'm not a talker.'

A pause lengthens, filled with the drone of the engine and the whoomphing of potholes.

Then she relents. 'You don't know how to sail?' she asks. He shakes his head. 'Would you like to learn?' She doesn't mean it. Paddy would never tolerate a novice on board. She wants to give John something, to make him feel wanted. She is surprised at the instinct.

'I couldn't care less about sailing,' he says.

'But I do,' she tells him. 'I care about sailing. If you want to learn I can get you a place on Paddy's boat. You'd be near me.'

'Do I get to see you in a bikini?'

They both laugh. She takes her left hand from the wheel and puts it on his forearm.

'Seriously. I'll see if Paddy would let you. He doesn't take to new kids.'

She is eight years older, a woman. He is a kid.

Chapter Five

Nora is watching a cat walk across her patio. The cat moves too slowly for reality, more like a jerky silent movie. She has no resilience. This is a cat dying, nine lives exhausted, never again to fall on her feet. She halts in mid stride, grinds her haunch down in a movement that reminds Nora of sex, and expresses three white crapcurrants. When she moves again she seems to walk on her claws, legendary poise teetering towards the ridiculous, an arthritic on high-heels. A rictus like a human smile distorts her face.

Who ever saw or heard of a cat dying of constipation? Nora wonders.

Later she finds the stiff little body in a clump of scutch under the cherry tree. She stands her up in rigor mortis, a patio pot as pedestal, a statue of her former self. The resemblance is exact.

By then it is evening. Mick is on his way home. He would be humming through closed teeth and tap-tapping the wheel. He would be preparing himself for another row, deciding where he would go for the dinner she will not have cooked, thinking of a shower.

Nora sets the cat up in full view of the patio window and turns the lights on. She sets a saucer of milk in front of her face but the crazy tilt of death makes the cat look permanently towards the sliding door, stare into the shade of the living room where Nora sits.

Ding dong he'll ring, she thinks. Ding dong although the bastard has his own key. What'll the neighbours say? They must maintain the fiction of a dutiful wife. She welcomes him home with a peck on the cheek. Hard day at the office love? Well it's been a hard day at the coalface too. A hard day in Survival Suburb. The heat is intense. The sun beating down relentlessly. Forty degrees in the shade. The orders come in from all over. Global orders. Uppers and downers keep me free. I could have gone under, taken the fall. It's been a hard day in Survival Suburb and the neighbours are no help. Silent women take children past my door. Men stare sideways through mirror sunglasses. They are thinking of having sex with me. What would it be like to have sex with a madwoman?

Different mister.

Ding dong.

I hate that bell. Why not change it for a buzzer? Why not hang a brass bell on a bit of rope. Not Survival Suburb's standard model, good old ding dong bell.

Ding dong.

Christ I never heard the car. Have a look at that fucking dead cat. It's going to knock him over. Mick on the floor? A whole new perspective on our marriage.

Ding dong.

Nora opens the door and Mick, as always, is struck by the extraordinary beauty, retained despite the punishment she gives it. Sometimes he thinks that she experiences no real suffering, locked up in the cells of her mind, no children to care for, no everyday mishaps. He thinks she is like a nun, insulated against the hard knocks of life but devastated by a tremor on the spiritual fault lines. Nora's fault lines open and close at irregular intervals and grind against each other and there is no grinding down. Every hard edge is there, identifiable, the same as when she first collapsed.

'Hard day at the office sweetheart?' She pecks him on the cheek. A rapid vicious peck like a hen pecking corn from gravel.

'Not so bad,' he says and steps inside. 'How are things?'

She closes the door and stands with her back to it. There is something triumphant about her features, a cold gleam in the eyes, a slight curl to the mouth. She has won some minor victory. It will involve him.

'Things are disgusting,' she says. 'Which thing are you enquiring about? Specifically?'

'I was only asking.' He puts his briefcase down on the hall table and is making for the kitchen.

'Come into the living room,' she says. 'I want to show you Tilly.'

She catches his wrist and leads him like a child into the room. She arranges him facing the window.

'Look. Tilly.'

Tilly on a patio pot staring at him. There is a saucer of milk in front of her. He is reminded suddenly of an acrobat he saw in a circus years ago. Poised in the centre of the high-wire, her face registered exactly the moment she knew she would fall. It was as though some sensitive instrument in the brain was calibrated for that moment. And something in his brain had recognised the look so that he knew, even before she began to tip outwards, that she was coming down. He tried to recall what happened to her, remembering only that she had broken a leg and an arm in the inadequate mattresses that were supposed to protect her. But no matter how hard he tried he could not remember her reaching the ground. In his memory she was poised for ever at the moment of equilibrium.

'She's much better today,' Nora says. 'I think my treatment's working.' Tilly was sick. Neither of them knew what she was sick of, but Nora had refused to take her to a vet. 'I'm sick,' she had said. 'The cat is sick. If my treatment works for me, it'll work for the cat.' Since then she had been assiduously crushing tablets and opening capsules, feeding Tilly the pharmacopoeia that she took herself: tranquillisers; analgesics; painkillers; laxatives; soporifics; hypnotics. Much of it had never been prescribed. Nora tracked it down through her 'sources', other women she met at gin mornings and in doctors' surgeries. They were a kind of secret sisterhood of drugs, sharing their supplies, phoning to discuss the latest prescription, comparing side-effects and contraindications.

'I gave her one of my little friends as a bit of a pick-me-up. I think she's feeling better. There's a spring in her step.'

Mick catches the dead eyes, the dull reflection of light from somewhere else. There is something about the dry circles that disturbed him. And the grin. Who ever heard of a cat grinning?

'She looks a bit better all right.'

The cat is unnaturally still.

'She won't eat though.'

Nora had gone through a phase of anorexia, eating virtually nothing, taking laxatives, lying about meals taken when he was out. The phase had passed now but for almost a year Mick believed she would starve herself to death.

'Are you a fanatic?' she asks suddenly. The kind of

question that terrified him. Nora's thought processes are mysterious to him, the strange outpourings of another world, a stream of anti-matters. Lucid days are rare.

'For God's sake. What's for dinner?' He swings away, opens the drinks cabinet. About an inch of Jameson in the bottle. No mixer.

'Only two kinds of people survive,' she tells him. 'The old and the fanatic. I think you're a fanatic.'

'Fuck off.'

'There's no dinner.'

'All right. I'll go out.'

'What about me?'

The cat draws his eyes again. There is no change in her posture. One paw is raised slightly. No, not raised. It is as though the shoulder itself is retracted pulling the paw upwards. Is there a fly on her nose?

'That cat is dead,' he says. He hopes it doesn't spark something in Nora. The cat is a favourite of hers.

'She was a junky,' Nora says. She laughs. 'The survival rate is small. This is Survival Suburb after all. Most of the females for miles around have learned how to survive. The weak go to the wall.'

'Nora what are you up to? What's going on now.'

'Crisis time,' Nora says.

'What crisis?' He is tired already, exhausted, worn down by their future and the past.

'I'm dying. I threw out your medals. They're gone in the bin.'

'Well Jesus Christ.'

'Mick Delany the County champeen!'

'You're sick, there's no doubt about it.'

'There is no doubt about it.'

A racket of white birds above the patio, twenty pigeons. Racing along some hidden ley-line, they wheel above the house once, twice. Their wing-claps penetrate the double glazing. Then they are gone. Their arrival and departure change things, the air clearer. Mick sits down and puts his head in his hands. She looks down at him. 'Poor petteen,' she says. She stands beside him and runs her hand down the back of his head to his neck. Two fingers catch the muscles there, working them gently.

'I can't help it,' she says.

'You have to go back to the doctor.'

'He's a bastard anyway.'

'Please Nora. Everything is getting destroyed.'

'Help me.'

'Christ! How can I help you. I'm in it myself. I'm destroyed with it. There's two of us here you know.'

'I want to die.'

He shakes his head, shaking her fingers off. 'No. That's not the way. That's a cowardly way.'

'Mick Delany the fearless corner-forward.'

'Fuck that.'

'That's all it is. Well I'm not a corner-forward. I want to die.'

He shakes his head again and gets up. In the fading light the rigid body on the patio pot looks like a child's toy. 'We have to bury that fucking cat.'

They eat at the Café Grec because everything else is booked out. Even the café has three tables with 'reserved' on them. An elderly man with a beard is the only other occupant, reading by the light of the guttering candle. The music was Nikis Theodorakis. A Greek version of Brendan Behan's music for *The Hostage*. He has heard it before. Nora says she recognises the other customer as a former lecturer of theirs. He does not, and he is aware of Nora's habit of seeing faces that she knew everywhere, of telling him their life stories. Once she had seen a nun and was able to tell him that she went to Biafra when the war started and was beaten up by both sides. Another time she pointed out a man as the judge who had fined her thirty pounds for not paying a parking ticket. She went up to him and berated him for doing it. The man threatened to call the guards. Mick dragged her away and never found out whether the story was true or not.

The elderly man with the beard eats in the American style, carefully cutting everything first, then using his fork only. She follows his knife-cuts studiously, relaxing when he settles down to eat.

'He always did that,' she says. 'He did his doctorate in Harvard.'

The Greek music stops abruptly and is replaced by the familiar monotony of Leonard Cohen's guitar-work. He hears the old song: 'Who by fire? Who by water? Who in the sunshine? Who in the night-time?' Too many questions. He wants them to put the Greek stuff back on but he knows if he asks for it she will stop him. She is listening intently, her eyes glazed. He wonders what the sounds do inside her head. Maybe she hears them differently, individually perhaps, or as a meaning-less jumble that she has to understand. Or perhaps the words describe what it is like in there, the unhappiness, the bleak uncertainty, the greyness.

For once the food is passable. Nora has a steak *au poivre* and eats with relish. He has darne of salmon. The salmon is dry but edible, the pink flesh brittle and fibrous at the same time. It is, he says, an achievement in its own right.

'Do you remember the party, Mick?' she asks. 'The one where you asked me to come home?'

He nods. She went with Paddy but Paddy disap-peared. They were both stoned out of their minds. Now Paddy is Mr Paddy Lynch, director of three companies, owner of two. And Paddy is married to Alice, years younger than him, a body like an angel, while he ends where he began, with Nora slowly dying on top of him, a stifling weight.

'I think of that sometimes. And the time we all went to the funeral. I was better then. That was before I got sick.'

'Oh yes,' Mick says. 'You were great then.'

'How did it start? I can't remember.'

Mick says that he doesn't remember either. But he does. Or at least he remembers the first episode when she had tried to hang herself. What caused it? He doesn't know. Until that time she was Crazy Nora, his unpredictable wife, the life and soul of a party. She would never agree to seeing a psychiatrist although her doctor had insisted. He supposed now that it was hereditary, that her parents had been the same. But they were dead when he met her, already dead by the time she was in university. Her sister paid for her education.

While they are drinking coffee Sandy Muldoon comes in. She hesitates at the door then walks boldly up to their table.

'Hi Mr Delany,' she says. Mick says 'Hi Sandy.'

'I didn't think you came in here,' Sandy says.

'I don't,' Mick says. 'It was the only place left. Friday night you know.'

'What did you think of the exhibition?'

'You know me,' he says. 'Not my cup of tea. I only go because I'm asked.'

'Still. Thanks for coming.' She passes on to sit at a table reserved for two.

'How do you know that one?' Nora hisses. 'I didn't know you knew her?'

'I do,' Mick says. 'She works in Cleary's gallery.'

'The Galleria Clary,' Nora says, mimicking Billy Cleary's pronunciation. 'She's a slut.'

'We get invitations at the office. Sometimes I go sometimes I don't. It's good for business.'

'I know for a fact that she's a slut. Someone told me she even got the clap. Syphilis. That's unusual nowadays.' Mick shrugs his shoulders. 'Don't start that,' he says. 'You don't know anything at all about her.'

'I pity you,' she says. 'I know for a fact she's the mistress of a friend of yours.'

'Who so?' he asks.

'I'm not telling you.'

'In my business facts like that don't count for much.' The insurance business, he means. He was not thinking of the office he managed, a whirlpool of gossip. Already he had heard that two of his secretaries had slept with him. He heard it from a colleague who had a gin and tonic too many at a convention hotel. And he had heard the story of his own drugs conviction applied to someone else.

'Oh. Do you know it's not true?'

'I know nothing about her.'

'"I didn't think you came here," she said. She knows about you.'

'What do I care.'

'She's watching you.'

'Let her.'

'She can't take her eyes off you.'

'Look, I hardly know her.'

That malicious spark in Nora's eyes. 'She idolises you because you played for the County. She's one of those women who fall for men with big thigh muscles.' Her laugh has the note of hysteria in it that he has come to recognise over the years. Not for the first time he wonders if he could have her committed. He had tried it before but that bastard Hennessy wouldn't take the bait. 'That's a big step to take,' he said. 'I wouldn't do it lightly.' And anyway she always managed to be perfectly rational and calm when a doctor was involved. She seemed to have a particular skill for making fools of them. In the end they always came away with the suspicion that there was something sinister behind his attempts to commit her, as though he were simply malicious.

Later, when Nora goes to the Ladies, Sandy smiles at him. He winks at her. She holds up the reserved sign and then points it at herself. He makes a puzzled face, but smiles innocuously. Then a student comes in. There is a little comedy of recognition. He goes to sit at another table. She beckons him to sit at hers. He sits down. He appears to be marvelling at the coincidence. Then Nora comes back out.

'The graffiti in the toilet is disgusting,' she says in a loud voice. 'It's all lesbian stuff. It's disgusting. All the things those women do.'

'The reason I want to die,' she tells him, 'is that I have a broken heart and I can't mend it.' She speaks like a little girl with a broken toy, a thin wandering voice, a falling cadence. 'I have a broken heart and I can't mend it.'

He swings the car into the drive and switches the engine off. He settles back in the seat. Who gives a shit, he thinks. Who gives a tinker's curse? Who gives a tuppenny fuck?

'I'm hopelessly in love with someone else, Mick. I'm sorry to have to tell you. For some years now. I'm so sorry Mick.'

'Get on with it,' he says. 'Who is it this time?'

She puts her hand on his leg. He feels his skin crawl under her touch, still game after all this time. 'It goes back years. All this time I've been faking everything. Our whole life was a lie.'

A neighbour (they hardly knew each other's names after four years) comes out to walk his dog. The neighbour stares resolutely ahead. No one looks at them, Mick knew, because everyone heard what they had to say to each other. In terms of sensory perception, the Delanys are an auditory perception rather than a visual one.

'Poor Paddy. Poor old Paddy,' she says. Mick groans. Not that. He has heard her stories about Paddy before. How she had slept with him to console him. How she had fallen in love with him but never dared to express it. How she had consoled him off and on since then, usually in their own bed. It is all fantasy, he knows, designed to hurt him. Paddy is too busy to have affairs, driven by a need for power and money that Mick believes would never be satisfied. Women play no part in that drive. They are incidentals.

'He should never have married her. That's the truth of it Mick. I told him that years ago. The day before the wedding I told him. Don't marry her Paddy, I said. She'll never love you.' She shakes her head at the thought of it. 'He wouldn't listen.' She is silent a moment, then she brushes away a tear. 'She can't love him of course. She's just not able to.' She takes a deep breath, holds it, then expels it, rushing her words out with it. 'She can't love him because of me.'

'What?' This is a new twist. Does she think that Alice Lynch knew about her imaginary liaisons with Paddy?

'She loves me.'

Mick whistles. 'That's a good one.'

'It's true. I could see it back then. She didn't like men. Will I tell you something?'

'Go on so,' Mick says wearily.

'This is a confession. Please treat it with respect.'

'I will.'

'We slept together.'

'Christ.'

'It's true.'

'It's always true, Nora. Every different story is true.

Even the ones that contradict each other.'

'I love her and she loved me. We slept together many times. She's a wonderful lover. All the things you couldn't be bothered doing. Her touch, it's just . . . perfect. She can make me happy. But she won't. She won't leave him. That's why I'm falling to pieces. That's why our marriage is falling to pieces. I want her.'

'I'm going to have a drink. You can come in if you like. Otherwise stay out here. I don't care.' He gets out of the car and slams the door.

'Men do it to themselves,' she calls. 'They ruin children and they turn them away from men for ever. Old men rape children! Priests do it even. Priests destroy people too.'

Jesus, Mick thinks, what is she working on now.

'I bought you a present,' she calls as he puts the key in the lock. 'It's on your bedside table.'

When he sits down on the side of the bed, glass of whiskey in hand, he sees it. A glass tree with hooks on the branches that hold little silver-framed photographs. She had cut up a group picture from college and hung his face and hers at the top, Paddy Lynch's below. Beneath that she had hung Alice Lynch's wedding portrait. There is a picture of Nora as an imp, a faded grey snap of a half-naked imp at the edge of the sea. The lower branches are festooned with pills, paper-clips carefully threaded through as hooks. He takes her picture down and looks at it. She was beautiful then.

'Christ,' he thinks. 'I'll have to bury that fucking cat.'

Chapter Six

Rain seems to hang in a single sheet from the coal-black sky to the footpath. Then wind comes and drives it along the road like smoke. Only where it brushes the ground is its true nature obvious. It seems to explode an inch above the surface so that there is a continuous fog there, suggesting doubts about the existence of anything truly terrestrial. John lingers on the steps of the hotel trying to decide whether the rain is a brief shower or something more permanent, whether or not he should wait it out or put his head down and brave it. The doorman has already exhausted his stock of wisdom about rain when Nora Delany rushes into the shelter of the hotel's canopy, shaking rainwater. He recognises her because Sandy had pointed her out to him, the desperate couple at the next table in Café Grec, her tear-stained face, a suggestion of faded beauty – burned rather than faded, like a leaf burned by spray, shrivelling slightly, slightly brown. Her husband he remembered from the gallery. The pinstriped man talking insurance to Paddy.

She slips on the second step and one leg splays out

awkwardly like a young foal. Her handbag and a plastic shopping bag fly out and land exactly at his feet. He helps her up, smelling something spirituous from her breath, stands her upright and asks if her leg is all right. It is fine, she is grateful for being picked up. She peers into his face. Does she know him? She is sure she does. He shakes his head. He does not know her, he says.

'But yes,' she says, pleased with herself. 'The boy from the Greek place.' *Boy* irritates him. 'I've seen you eating there a lot. You're always on your own. Except once. I remember. That gallery girl was with you.'

'Yes,' he says. 'You're right. You do know me.'

'Nora Delany,' she says, transferring her bags to her left hand and sticking the right one out at an angle. 'Let me stand you a drink – no, I insist. You rescued me. You're not going anywhere until this stops anyway.'

They gravitate towards the dark cubicle of the bar, and are surrounded by cheap pine and old pottery whiskey jars. A ship under full sail is depicted in a large print over their heads. The ash-tray is white, heavy and full of spent cigar butts. His is a pint of Smithwicks. She has something small. Probably gin.

'So,' she says, pushing her coat away from her and knocking the plastic bag in the process. 'Tell me all about yourself. I love meeting people.'

He laughs. 'I'm a student, that's all.'

'Not much. A student of what?'

'Philosophy.'

'In that case,' she says, 'I should ask you what is the meaning of life.' She begins to giggle uncontrollably. He laughs again. 'You'll have to try Monty Python for that one,' he says.

'Only, my doctor is a great believer in the golden mean. As the meaning of life. If you can get the right combination of uppers and downers you won't ever have to experience anything at all.'

He stops laughing suddenly and fiddles with his glass, adjusting it on the beer mat, then spreading an oozing spillage so that it has the shape of an animal. She watches the frothy pool develop, conscious that her despair has some unforeseen effect on him.

'I upset you,' she says. 'I didn't mean to.'

'That's all right,' he says. 'Is it really as bad as all that?' She makes a face. 'Not presently. I have the combination right I think. I'm quite up. Very up as a matter of fact. Now that I mention it, maybe I'm too up. Oh Jesus. There's always another side to it, isn't there?'

'I don't know.'

'There is. It would be all right if I – if I felt badly about it I suppose.'

'Don't you feel bad?'

She thinks for a moment. 'Faded,' she says. 'I feel faded and – and neutral. That's not much is it?'

'I don't know. I'm a philosophy student. Not psychology.'

'It's the same thing. Around the edges anyway.'

He smiles the benign smile of someone who knows more. 'I'm afraid they're completely different. Even around the edges.'

'Postgraduate?'

He realises she is changing the subject, grasps at the proffered escape with a will. 'Yes. That's right. I suppose I must look a bit old all right. Yes, postgraduate. Philosophy as a matter of fact.'

'Thesis?'

'Yes. Kierkegaard. Søren Kierkegaard. Ever heard of him?' She shakes her head. 'Søren Kierkegaard,' he is almost chanting from memory, 'proposed to Regina Olsen in 1840, however he soon came to believe that marriage was incompatible with his vocation to be a writer. This vocation he believed to be a mission from God.' He stops. 'Did I give it enough irony? I don't know if I can.'

'Are you writing a thesis about his marriage?'

'Non-marriage. No. It's on my mind at the moment that's all.'

'Who's the lucky girl?'

'Who is the happiest except the unhappiest, and what is life but madness, and love but vinegar in the wound. Kierkegaard.'

'Jesus.' Her face pinched, surprised by anger, her mouth bared, back arched in fury, like an animal about to pounce.

'Not exactly.'

'He sounds like a pretentious shit. A pain.' She spits it out. Shit! like that. Angry and hurt.

'Kierkegaard? A sensitive shit. Religious too. I think I made a mistake in picking him.' He swallows a considerable amount of beer. 'I think I should apply for a change.'

'I would. That crap!'

'I should have gone for someone upbeat and positive like Camus. *The Plague*. Now there's a positive book. And of course Camus committed suicide. There's an affirmation of life for you. Bate that, as they say at home.'

The bar is filling up with businessmen in wet suits, women in waxed overcoats and funny hats, shaking umbrellas and opening them out and leaving them propped like skewed toadstools in the foyer. The manager fusses over them in a grey pinstripe coat, trying to persuade them to close up the umbrellas and hand them in at the cloakroom. The bar is beginning to smell like the cellar of a pub, musty and damp; or like a place where the air was still and clothes dried on racks over days or weeks. Men are calling in high-pitched voices, signalling with fingers for the number of drinks – two pints there Slim, a gin and tonic two vodkas and a pint of Murphy's, a large whiskey large now, hot toddy two.

There is a suggestion of jocular panic as though they had survived an ambush. The women linger on the outskirts of the crowd. They watch each other, occasionally chat, wait for the fistfuls of glasses of clear liquid. Secretaries. Wives. Colleagues. The men do the ordering, pay the man.

'I think I'll kill myself too,' she says. 'Really. It's probably the best I can do.' She shrugs and smiles weakly. 'I had religion once. Not Catholicism. That comes with mother's milk. You don't *get* Catholicism. But I joined a sect, what they call a cult, when I was in college first. They had a monastery, a commune really, on an island. I used to go there during the holidays. The papers called us The Screamers, but they called most of the cults screamers. It was a popular name at the time.' He laughs, interested. 'Anyway, as it happens, one of the things they encouraged us to do was scream. I never stopped. That's my problem.'

The crowd from the bar surges and a girl in a blue miniskirt steps back against their table, her upper thighs bulging briefly against the pine. 'Sorry,' she says. He notices that she is wearing glossy tights that make her legs look artificial, varnished. It makes him think of Alice, her long legs lying on his. She had no hair on her legs. Did she shave?

'We had some suicides too. The cult leader said, I quote, suicide is an affirmation of the godhead. Did you ever hear such shit?' He shakes his head. Pretentious shit, he says. Joke theology.

'But still. I think about it. There were times even then when I thought seriously about it. I used to think it would be a gesture. Now I don't care about gestures.'

'A gesture would be a bit pointless. You'd never see the effect. It should have a meaning. Or it should be the result of intolerable circumstances.'

'Like what's his name? Which one was his?'

'Who?'

'The philosopher that committed suicide.'

Panic grips him with the realisation that this is not a disinterested discussion, not philosophy. 'Meaning, I think,' he stammers. 'It would have had to be meaning. I'm not sure. I'm guessing. I don't know much about Camus.'

'How did he do it?'

He shakes his head and tries to concentrate.

'I – I'm not sure. Car crash I think.' Suddenly he is backtracking, shocked. 'I don't think they're certain of it anyway. I don't think anybody really knows for sure. It could have been an accident. Apparently he drove very fast. A demon on the roads. French of course.'

'The French are nearly as bad as the Italians.'

'So I'm told.'

'My husband was a champion hurler. Did you know that? Very fast.'

'Hurling is – a very fast game.'

'Played for the County. He was very strong.'

He says nothing, wondering where this information is leading.

'Now he's the manager of an insurance office. I suppose it was predictable enough. Before I married him he told me this would be the way. I should have believed him. The bastard was only telling the truth all along.'

'Nothing is as neat as that. Life is messy.' He is thinking about one night with Alice, then the furtive sequels: the striation of his life into lines of lust, lines of love, desperation, work. How a single line of life had forked, faulted, blundered. How a single phrase could make him frantic with desire. Hours of work lost to dreams. To see her and to love her is the same thing, and the same thing repeats itself endlessly, Kierkegaard said. And he is possessed by the thought for half a night. To see and to love. To have had and not to have.

'Messy. A car crash would be messy. And you might survive.'

'Will you have another one?' He is desperately hoping she will say no, remember that she has an appointment (except that it is after office hours: nothing is open), that she has to go home and cook the dinner. He wants to go out into the rain, to let it fall, to choke in it. 'I will so,' she says. 'Vodka on the rocks.'

He struggles through the crowds, walking through ordinary conversations like a sleepwalker. 'He missed the conversion—' 'Ballocks to her anyway—' 'Turbo GX or something—' 'Good God! A hundred K? That much—'

'Pint of Smithwicks and a vodka on the rocks please.' He wonders if people who are actually going to commit suicide ever talk about it. Perhaps the fact that she is discussing it means that she wouldn't do it. On the other hand, people always say that there are warning signs. But she doesn't even know him. Should he phone her husband and say: 'I had this strange conversation with your wife . . .' Besides, he doesn't know her husband's phone number.

When he comes back she is crying quietly. He puts her glass on the table in front of her and goes to sit on the far side. He wonders whether he might have a clean tissue in his pockets and decides that he probably has none at all. Then he considers getting a paper napkin from the bar. They always keep a supply there for people who want cocktails. He saw one of the barmen shaking the stainless steel bottle earlier, and the glass with the long stem and a napkin twisted on it. In the end she picks up her handbag and spends a minute opening it and staring into it. He catches a glimpse of what looks like a fruitcake of pills, all jammed together in a loose pocket. Then she pulls out a packet of Posies, extracts one sheaf deftly with painted fingernails, and blows her nose.

'The funny thing is,' she says, and blows her nose

again. 'The funny thing is that it's all the wrong way round. I went to college too you know. There was a time when I used to enjoy going to exhibitions with Mick. Now, all those things. Poisoned. It's the wrong way round. Everything that's supposed to make life better, more beautiful. It's all blackened. Ridiculous. Futile.'

'It's not all that bad,' he says. 'Cheer up now.' He sees himself at that moment as the fatuous friend, the banal advice-giver. Cheer up. Get a grip on yourself. Pull yourself together. Into each life some rain must fall. He wonders how he can be so unprepared, despite all his reading, for the appearance of uncomplicated despair.

And she says, 'Jesus, is that all you can come up with? A fucking master of philosophy!'

He is stung nevertheless. 'If I knew I was going to have your problems dumped on me, I'd have gone in for psychology. Or I'd have gone for Thomas Aquinas. He had some ideas on suicide.'

'Fuck you.'

'Fuck yourself.'

They sit in silence for a while. He thinks he should get up and walk out. Can he stick another hour of her angst? But he half believes her. She could actually be thinking of suicide. She certainly seems depressed enough for it. He feels responsible, as though the mention of Albert Camus had triggered it, though he knows that was too trivial a cause for this.

'I think I'll do it here,' she says. He blinks first in surprise, then laughs, unable to contain the flood of relief. 'Here? In the bar? You'd be a huge hit!' She's not serious.

She shakes her head slowly. 'Upstairs,' she says. 'I think I'll book a room.'

She is bluffing, he thinks. A pitch for his sympathies. This is too dramatic. 'Why not,' he says. 'That's a good idea. Why mess up the bedroom at home.'

'Come up with me,' she says. 'Help me.'

'Ah,' he says, waving a finger of admonition. 'Then it wouldn't be suicide would it? It would be something else. I think they call it assisted suicide now. In the old days they would have said murder. Euthanasia if you were sick.'

'I am.'

'Only insofar as we all are. The world is sick. For those whose youth is past there exists no sanctuary to absorb their melancholy.' He is pleased with himself, pulling that quotation out of the air. But who said it? He can't remember.

'Come upstairs with me. Just to talk. Away from the noise. I'll do it later. After you're gone.'

He almost laughs in her face. 'I'm not usually propositioned by suicides.'

Her face hardens. 'Are you ever propositioned by anyone?'

'Look, I suggest you go home and sleep it off. You'll be better in the morning.'

She appears to shrivel, a physical wrinkling inwards of her shoulders, her hands, her knees. Her face seems to fold inwards. She becomes physically smaller. 'I'll be better in the morning,' she repeats.

'Anybody sitting here?' A slope-shouldered blond, a rugby head, pointed and tight-cropped. No, John says. Yes, she says. It is a private conversation actually. Did he mind. He recoils and gazes at them with mock-awe.

'Well shag it all,' he cries. 'What do we have here? Baby-snatching?'

'Leave them alone Damien,' a girl says. 'Your one is upset. Look at her.' Damien looks at her and turns away abruptly, his broad backside to them now, a white shirt loosed from the belt of his trousers intended to suggest wildness. 'Some fucking funeral that is anyway,' they hear him say before the crowd brays and someone begins to tell a story that has them all leaning forward, their drinks poised at an unnatural angle.

'Well?'

'Well what?'

'Come upstairs. I'll pay for the room.'

Now he looks at her closely for the first time. She has been a beauty, still carries herself like that. Her eyes gaze frankly into his, but there are dark saucers around them, and tight near-vertical lines around her mouth. 'Who exactly are you?' he asks. 'What's your name again? I forgot.'

'Nora,' she says. 'What's yours?'

'John.'

'Dear John,' she says, and chuckles. 'A dear john letter.'

'I won't come up with you Nora.'

'All right.' Her face shows no sign of disappointment, no change at all.

'I think you should see a doctor.'

'I see doctors all the time. Even when I'm asleep.'

'About your depression.'

'Oh that! That's nothing. I have my little friends.' She taps her bag. 'They pick me up on my way down. That's a song. Before your time.' She sings in a coy, slightly nasal American voice, 'Pick me up on your way dow-own.' He feels her foot on his under the table. 'How 'bout it cowboy? Pick me up on your way down?' Her foot slides up his calf.

He gets up suddenly, shaking the table and almost unbalancing what is left of his pint. Now the room seems to be full of prop-forwards and bimbos, the walls patterned with shipping prints, tall full-sailed vessels leaning purposefully into sepia-tone seas. It occurs to him that he is the only person in the hotel who doesn't know where he is going. Even Nora knows that she is bound to die. 'I have to go,' he tells her. 'I forgot. I'm supposed to be meeting someone.'

'Going so soon? Hear that folks,' she says, raising her voice. The rugby crowd spin round, mouths open, eyes searching for the angle, leaving the storyteller in mid-sentence. They beam at her and watch him as he makes his way around the edge, avoiding people on stools, knots of men holding small glasses. They whistle after him, and someone calls, 'Forward pass! Forward pass!'

He breaks through into the foyer and finds the smell of damp again, the doorman staring balefully at a cluster of newly sprouted umbrellas. 'Bad night,' the doorman says, jerking a thumb at the smoking road. 'I'd say it won't clear up at all tonight.' The rain still blanks everything except the headlights of passing cars. This time he does not hesitate.

Chapter Seven

She thinks: ding dong. If I went up to him now and opened my legs he would fuck me for all he's worth. It's as simple as that. Ding dong. He goes to the office in his BMW. He comes back in the evening. He plays golf on Saturday (natural progression from hurling) and drinks in the clubhouse on Sunday. Delany the Boring. This is the end of all corner-forwards. Athletes go to seed as surely as women and cats. The light dies in them the same as it does for the rest of us. The man with the long arms and belly like steel is the paunchy forty-five-year-old practising his putting in slippers. She remembered his hair streaked back as though the pace of his hurling had flattened it, his eyes focused on the ball at the tip of his hurley, his legs going like pistons. Then the crazy, angular flip, the twist and pull, and the thock of the *sliotar* lifting into the air, curving inwards and downwards to drop between the posts. That was the winning point. Mick Delany.

She slips into the driver's seat and fumbles her bag open. Yes she has the spare keys. She starts the car and reverses out on to the road. She sees him pull the curtain back, sees him seeing her. She lowers the window and waves two spread fingers at him in the darkness. Then she takes off.

The BMW goes well and the automatic makes driving easier. She drives fast, cornering noisily, accelerating even on short straights. She heads for the country, pointed west. In five minutes she has left the suburbs. Now the country roads flash past at the edge of light. Houses too. She goes through an empty village. She swings north towards the higher ground. The roads become narrower. Trees overhang. She feels the wheels losing their touch on the wet margins, the car waltzing from time to time. She comes to a fork in the road and takes the right-hand junction, quickly realising that she has made the wrong choice. The road deteriorates, bouncing the car, narrows so that thistles are slashing the windscreen from the ditches, briars snapping along the bodywork. It ends in a derelict farmyard, the smell of cowshit and dead rats. A fox barking.

She switches off the engine and gets out.

She lets her eyes get used to the gloom. She has her handbag under her arm.

The farmhouse has no glass in the windows. Its thatch collapsed inwards, grass and briars growing through. There are some small outhouses. Only one is roofed. She is drawn to that. She stands at the door staring into the pitch blackness. The ground underfoot is dry, a sort of thin crust crumbling as she scuffs it. The darkness is pungent, smelling of rot and shit. The doorway expands before her, a vortex drawing her in. She looks back at the car once. She shakes her head. She steps through.

Dawn filters out along the eastern sky. It is a thin pink dawn, cool, moist. A fine sheath of gossamer has evened out the rough grass and stony outcrops. They gleam like steel filaments. Paddy strides through it wearing a wax jacket, a bandoleer of cartridges and a pair of green Wellington boots. He whistles. He has borrowed a dog for the day. He watches her sniffing around and nosing into the wet rushes and thinks, 'That bitch is useless. I shouldn't have bothered.'

His way is uphill, away from the Merc parked in a quiet bye-road. He leans forward a little, watches his feet, and thinks about killing. He has come out to escape the snare of offers and bids, buy-outs and take-overs that has besieged the office. A memorandum of agreement sits on his desk that will enable him to offload the least profitable component of his portfolio of companies in advance of the Stock Exchange flotation of Micro Solutions. But the agreement is on a knife-edge, the purchaser on the verge of finding out just how unprofitable the company is.

A snipe rises out of the watery valley on his left and is gone almost before he can raise his head. He hears the clatter and whirr and watches the characteristic zigzag pattern of the bird's flight. The bitch looks up at him.

He unslings the Purdey and puts two cartridges in. He closes the gun again, sensing the beautiful action that cocks the hammers and puts the safety catch in place. The gun has been away for repairs and Paddy has felt bereft.

Now he stalks along with the gun held low across both hands. He makes encouraging noises for the bitch who dives wildly about nosing everything and going off in different directions after every half-scent. Paddy watches her antics and clicks his tongue from time to time.

A boy setting snares comes through the farmyard. It is Saturday morning. He sees the car and suspects that there is someone asleep in it. He hopes it is a naked man and woman. Or better again, a naked woman. He tiptoes up to the window and looks in. There are no people inside, but the doors are open. That must mean that the owner is nearby. The next thing he thinks is that this is someone coming to buy the old place. Old Patsy Carroll must be after dying in the County Home and his daughter in America is selling the land. His father would want to know about that.

But there is no sign of a man in a three-piece suit, no auctioneer, no BMW driver. Now he thinks the car might have been left by joyriders, but they usually burn them out to get rid of the fingerprints. Besides, the car was in perfect shape apart from a few scratches. Joyriders usually wreck their cars.

He begins to look around. He checks the windows of the house. No one is there. The sight of the rusty old iron bed with the rat-eaten mattress restores the thought of sex to him. He begins to hope again that he will come upon a city couple rutting in the house or one of the sheds. He makes straight for the roofed shed.

At first, before his eyes adjust, he thinks he has found a dead animal. The land is poisoned and sometimes cats and dogs find the poison and die. He sees her hair, bunched in the light of the door and thinks he has found a dead cat. Then he sees that it is a woman lying in one corner, her handbag clutched to her side, her legs slightly spread. He thinks she is alive but asleep. He sees that she is a looker, a real fine half. He goes in and squats down beside her, admiring the full curve of her breasts, the elegance of her face. He wonders if it is possible to have sex with someone in their sleep. Then he tries to wake her up. He shakes her gently by the arm but she does not move. He puts his hand in front of her mouth but can detect no breath. He feels her cheek and it is cold. He knows now that she is dead. The realisation comes to him easily. He does not panic. He has been squatting beside her for some time. He is not going to run away now.

He knows he should go home and tell his mother. She would phone the guards and the priest. Instead he stays where he is, savouring this first proximity to beauty. He thinks about what could have driven such a woman to her death and the thought perplexes him. Surely someone like her must have everything. He thinks of the BMW parked outside.

He wants to lift her skirt and look at her, pull aside her blouse and see what the breasts of a beauty look like. He feels desperate, as though this may be his last chance. What kind of women will I pull? he asks himself. No one like this anyway.

He sees that she has a wedding ring on the hand that clutches the handbag. The bag is open, two plastic bottles visible inside. He looks more closely at the bottles and understands. He looks into her sleeping face and thinks about death. He thinks of the death of a neighbour, the face stretched over bones, bony hands folded on the sheets, a rosary wound into the fingers. He runs his hand across hers but is frightened by the cold. It's not like the cold of stone or metal.

He stands back now, aware suddenly that his prick has grown big in his trousers. 'God forgive me,' he says. It is automatic. He blesses himself and says an act of contrition aloud. It is for her, not for himself.

He goes out and opens the car. The keys are still in the ignition. He sits in and opens the glovebox. He shuts it again. The sun has come out, heat beating through the windscreen at him. The smell of warm leather, other people's clothes. The dead woman had no smell, he thinks.

A pheasant rises explosively out of the ditch. Paddy swivels round, bringing the gun to his shoulder and easing off the safety catch in a single smooth motion. He sights the bird and his finger tightens on the front trigger. He feels the secret tightening of cams and gears, senses the coming explosion. But the bird is out of range already. His finger loosens again. A shot now would be pointless and would only alert anything else nearby. He lowers the gun and sees the bird disappear behind a distant hedge, its flight path tending gradually downwards.

He swings left, climbing higher. The ground is rougher here, limestone showing through in places like bone wearing through a thin skin. He pauses for a time at the walls of a derelict house and wonders how the inhabitants eked out a living. The only signs of farming he has seen are a few sheep lower down, grazing between stones. The bitch lies at his feet, her tongue dangling like a loose belt, a hurt look in her eyes. He has decided to ignore her.

He eats a sandwich and drinks from the coffee-flask. The coffee tastes burnt and the sandwiches are dry and papery. He moves off again, noting that it is already past noon. 'I'll give it an hour,' he says. He likes this outward movement. Ideally he would like to leave the car somewhere, walk for six hours and have a different car ready at the other end. Paddy dislikes returns.

He climbs laboriously over a gate, the first he has had to cross, and sees that he is coming into arable land, civilisation. A dirty grey stubble covers the field. Ahead of him is a slight valley with a run-down farmyard at its bottom. He is surprised to see the garish colours of an ambulance as well as three cars. People are moving around down there. Paddy thinks some old bastard from

the hills has died, some dried-up bachelor whose constipated grasp of land and money sustained him to a ripe
old age. He looks around and notes that the nearest
neighbour is more than a mile away.

He hears the sudden clatter of wings and foliage and
knows instinctively that a pheasant has risen. He swings
around and sights towards the sound, finds the bird, aims
off a little, aware, even as he squeezes the trigger, that
the bitch has finally done something right. After the gun
goes off he sees the spatter of feathers that means a hit
and watches the bird go down awkwardly. Whatever
grace a pheasant in flight has is annulled in its clownish
death. He breaks the gun instinctively, as he strides
towards the fall, and slots another cartridge down the
barrel. He closes the gun, slips the safety catch off and
whistles for the bitch.

The pheasant is lying in an awkward bundle in the
stubble. The bitch stands three feet away, one front paw
held up to her chest, her nose pointing at the obvious.
Paddy ignores her.

The boy hears the shot as the stretcher is rolled into the
ambulance. He thinks that is one less for him. He feels
the hard wires of the snares in his trouser pocket. The
guard is on his radio trying to contact the station but he
is out of range. The air is full of the hissing static. The
boy's mother and father are talking in undertones to the
driver of the ambulance. All three stare at the boy as they
talk. But the boy turns away and thinks of the woman's
body in the shadows. He thinks, that would be what a
woman would look like in the morning, waking in bed.
So cool and beautiful.

Chapter Eight

The doctor's waiting room is cold despite the scorching heat of the radiator. Except for a series of graduate parchments (*Hic testantur* . . . a whole letter in Latin adding up to the qualifications of Samuel Ignatius Hennessy to deal in life and death), a Sacred Heart calendar and a wooden picture of Padre Pio, stigmatic hands joined in prayer, looking down at the suffering, the walls are bare. Sandy sits by the radiator, flicking through *Hello!* magazine. The only other person is an elderly man whose left leg never stops jigging up and down, as though his metabolism cannot cope with silence and expresses itself in the manic rhythm. Sandy has a low armchair, he a high hard kitchen chair. 'Sure I'd never get out of that,' he tells Sandy when she offers it to him, leaving her to wonder whether gravity, old age or comfort would be the glue that held him down. The lives of the pointless rich pass between them, he staring at the pictures upside down from his eminence. The blonde women and boys. The soft sweaters and shaggy dogs. The family portraits. The brocades. The silk. The library shelves. The topiary. The fountains. The honourables embarking on second or third relationships. Partners. Coy references to beds. And princesses patronising cripples, refugees, cats' homes, the elderly deaf, the diseased, the impoverished. *Hello!* is another world.

'Next.'

She puts the magazine back on the table and realises, too late, that after all there were a few old *Time* magazines. She goes through the door and finds herself in a large room with a couch on one side, a screen standing closed beside it, a large desk with an office chair and two ordinary plastic chairs. There are charts of all kinds on the walls, all of them advertising drugs or appliances. The notepad on his desk says Nurofen.

The doctor is already seated. He pulls a drawer open and takes out a pad. He places the pad in front of him, positions it with both of his palms so that it is square on to the table. Then he picks up a pair of reading glasses and flicks them open. It is a deft flick, a parlour trick almost. He puts the glasses on and picks up a pen.

'Yes.'

Sandy doesn't know what to say.

'What can I do for you?'

She tells him that she has just started a full-time job working for a gallery and she has found a flat. Since she'll be living here she has decided to find a GP in the area and since he is the nearest to her, well, that's why she came.

'I see.'

'I'm hoping you'll take me on as a patient.'

'I see. No problem of course. But is there something wrong with you?'

Sandy is hesitant. 'Well . . . I've been to see our GP at home—'

'Yes?'

'About a complaint. I suppose I should have brought a letter.'

'Helpful.'

'I suppose it would.'

'Well, I can write to him.'

'He wasn't really able to do much for me.'

'Oh yes?'

'Not much really. In fact you could say he was baffled.'

'Baffled?'

The doctor reaches up and lifts his glasses on to the top of his head. He pinches the top of his nose with his thumb and index finger and then rubs the fingers into his eyes. Then he lets the glasses slip down again, and magically they are exactly in place in front of his watery pupils.

'Now miss . . ?' Pen poised above the pad.

'Sandy. Sandy Muldoon.'

'Sandy?'

'Geraldine.' He writes her name down in a box at the top of the form. He does not ask her how Geraldine has mutated to Sandy and she does not volunteer the simple fact that it is the colour of her hair.

'Address?'

She gives him her address and date of birth and various other details.

'Now, medical history. What about this complaint.'

She describes the pain she felt, pointing to a spot between her pubic hair and her navel.

'A burning pain,' he writes. She nods. It was like a fire in her belly, she says. Hot. Burning.

'I see.' He looks up from the pad and stares at her. Now she notices that he has small eyes, pinpoints almost, a small nose and a small mouth. But his hands are fat. Like a farmer or a mason. He wears a shiny blue suit and his shirt-sleeves are grey around the rims. His tie has some kind of a club symbol on, like a pair of hurleys crossed, or golf-clubs, a thing that might be a spider or a crown poised above them.

'What gallery is this you're working in?' he asks. She is taken by surprise. It is as though his mind has been elsewhere all this time.

'Galleria Clary,' she says.

He smirks. 'Clary. My wife and I, we get invited to that place. We bought a picture there last year as a matter of fact. As an investment. As far as art goes, we wouldn't know art from a telephone pole.' An amusing thought strikes him and his lips twitch. 'In fact, now, you could get a telephone pole. I wouldn't be a bit surprised if someone brings in a pole one of these days. A pole with a dab of paint on it.' He wheezes laughter. She smiles. 'That's modern art as far as I'm concerned. I read someplace that some fellow brought in a dead sheep. I have a feeling I saw you there all right. At the gallery. Sometime.'

'You were at the Bredin exhibition.'

'I was. I remember that. Anyway?'

'Well, that's it really.'

'Any particular pattern?'

'Yes,' she says. She is conscious that the answer to this question gives ground away, that it will weaken her case. 'When a period starts. That's the worst time. Sometimes I have to stay in bed. I nearly missed my finals over it.'

'Finals?'

'Arts. History and mathematics.'

'And mathematics?'

'So I nearly missed it.'

'Maths isn't a girl's subject.'

'Not generally, no.'

'And is there a difference between the pain of the period and this . . . complaint you have?'

'I get it nearly every time.'

'Where?'

She points to the same place. It is a fleeting gesture, indicative of her fear.

'And what did your doctor make of it?'

Sandy searches her mind for the phrases she has been preparing. She cannot say what her doctor made of it or she will lose this battle completely. Desperation sharpens her mind and she manages to grasp a noncommittal sentence.

'He said it needed further investigation.'

'Did he send you to a specialist?'

Panic. 'He said I didn't need to.' Wrong. That was the wrong answer.

'Didn't need it.' The fingers push the glasses up again. The eyes are rubbed. The glasses fall into place. 'I see.'

'I have to stay in bed with it often,' she says.

'Well we'd better examine you. If you'd go behind that screen there and take your clothes off.'

'All my clothes?'

'Well, you could leave your underpants.'

Sandy goes behind the screen. It is not big enough to hide her and at first she tries to undress without leaning forward. After removing her T-shirt and jeans she decides to extend the screen. It is mounted on wheels that squeak as they move. It extends in jerks. She is intensely aware of the fact that her bare feet are exposed below the screen where the frame is a few inches above ground. She removes the rest of her clothes and stares bleakly at the couch for a moment.

The couch is old, brown leather, cracked and broken in places, horse-hair showing at the corners. She supposes it is an heirloom, perhaps bequeathed to the doctor by his father. It is slightly tilted and a sheet of tissue covers where her head and back will be. She steps into the open and stretches out on the couch.

'Fine.' The doctor gets up from his desk, his back still turned and pauses for a moment, looking at a poster or calendar in front of the desk. Then he turns towards her. 'I hope that couch isn't too cold,' he says. She knows from the way he says it that he says this to everyone. It is automatic, weary.

He stands beside the couch and looks down at her breasts. 'Now where exactly is this pain?' His hands hang loosely by his side. She sees that he has a broad wedding band and that the fat of his fingers bulge around it. He wears an Omega watch, the tiny roman numerals clear as pieces of steel, the second hand sweeping smoothly through them.

She makes the gesture again, her hands fluttering. Then she realises that the gesture is neurotic. She puts her right hand on her abdomen, just above the elastic of her pants. 'About here,' she says, thinking of the crippling pain, trying to remember the exact epicentre of the events that punctuate her life, that turn her into a weeping victim for three days every month. The quake that pulls her down.

'I'll have to . . . just . . . put this down,' he says, putting his hands behind her head to the raised back of the couch. 'If you'd just sit forward for a second. That's it. Now lie down.' Sandy finds herself stretching slowly backwards, extending her body out. She feels her breasts tightening, coming erect, her stomach muscles hardening. Then she is flat on her back staring at the ceiling. She can see up his nostrils from there, the snarls of hair like a cluster of leggy insects. He looks at her again, his eyes travelling from her breasts to her knees. Then he lifts his hands and rubs them together vigorously. 'Cold hands,' he says, but the movement seems gleeful to her, like a child anticipating a feast.

'Now.' He puts one hand on her stomach and looks into her eyes. 'Not too cold?' She shakes her head. He increases the pressure. His hand feels heavy but not hard. She imagines she can separate the sensation made by the heel of his hand from that of his fingers. 'Anything?' She shakes her head. 'Pain?' She shakes her head again. His hand is moving around her abdomen, pressure increasing wherever it goes. 'Discomfort?'

'A little.'

'Where? Exactly?'

'There.'

'Here?'

She nods.

'Anything here?' She shakes her head. 'Or here?'

'No.'

'I see.'

He has taken his hand away. Now he is looking at her pants. He lifts the edge of it with both hands and peels it back a little. He puts his hand on the mound of her pubic hair and pushes. She winces.

'Sore?'

'Yes. A bit.'

'I see.'

He does not take her panties off. He puts his hand on the inside of her thighs and pushes them slightly apart. She separates her legs. He touches various spots. Once or twice she winces.

'Do you know there's a bit of bruising down here?' he asks. She can hear it in his voice. Disapproval. Contempt.

'I saw it,' she says.

'Recent?'

'Last Sunday morning. In the toilet. I noticed it then.' Light grey, fading fast. She knew they were there.

'I see.'

'I think the sore place here,' she touches her pubic hair, 'is the same thing. Not related to the pain at all.'

'No. I was thinking that.'

'Something else completely.'

'Well, if you'd like to get dressed now.'

'Is that all?'

'For now anyway. Dress up. And sit over.'

She goes behind the screen again, almost laughing now at the incongruity of lying naked in front of him for five minutes, letting him touch her wherever he wanted and now ducking behind a screen to put her clothes back on.

When she is dressed again she sits on the same plastic chair.

'Miss Muldoon.'

'Yes doctor.'

'Tell me this now. What exactly did your doctor say about this pain?'

'What I told you.'

'I see. Did he order any tests?'

'Blood tests. An X-ray. Some sort of a scan.'

'And nothing showed?'

She shakes her head.

'I'm going to ask you some questions now and you don't have to answer them. You understand that? You don't have to answer them. But if I'm going to get to the bottom of this I have to eliminate certain things.'

'OK.'

'Well, to start with. Those marks on your thighs. I think if I carried out an internal examination I might find bruising.'

'Maybe.'

'Would you like to tell me anything about that?'

She looks away. She finds herself staring at a weighing scales with a wicker basket on it. She wonders what a baby weighs. How many babies have been weighed on that basket, impossibly flimsy to hold the slightest human form.

'I see. Now this pain. How long has it been going on?'

'Since I was eleven or twelve.'

'I see. I notice from the history you gave me that you said your father and mother separated about that time.'

Oh no, she thought. I will never get out of this circle. 'It has nothing to do with that!'

'No. No. I'm sure it hasn't. Did you miss your father?'

'No.'

'I see. Why was that now?'

'You said I didn't have to answer the questions.'

'No. But, you know, if I'm going to make any headway—'

'I didn't like him that's all.'

'That's unusual in a daughter.'

'I did psychology in first year doctor. I know all about the Electra Complex.'

'You're ahead of me there,' the doctor said. A cold smile formed and died on his face. 'I'm not familiar with the term. What I'm asking you really is could there be a connection between the pain and the, the loss? That's all.'

'Look he wasn't abusive or anything. Not an alcoholic or anything. He never beat me up. He never beat my mother up either. He just left, that's all.'

'Was it someone else?'

'Yes.'

'I see. Was it someone you knew? Or someone your mother knew?'

Sandy shrugs. It is a tight angry shrug. Her face has set into an ugly child's sulk.

'He was a doctor.'

The doctor blinks then lifts his glasses, pinches his eyes and drops them into place.

'Well. Is that important?'

'No. I just thought I'd say it. It was a patient that he left with. He almost got disbarred for it. But she was old enough. Over the age of consent. Her parents kept quiet in the end. And the what do you call it? Medical Council. They issued a reprimand or something. Slapped him on the wrist. But he didn't lose his right to practise.'

Eleanor is her name. She has four children now. Sometimes she sends a postcard of them. North of Montreal. They can speak Canadian French and English. He works in a hospital where most of his patients are lumberjacks and farmers. She says that trauma is his speciality. He has saved more lives than she would like to mention. He misses Sandy. Will she ever come over and visit a while?

'I see. Now these bruises.'

'None of your business.'

'Fine. Fine. But what I'm wondering is, it wasn't force was it? I notice you have a bruise on your neck too, just above the clavicle. And, am I right in saying that the shadow on your cheekbone is another one, fading away a bit. An older one?'

'Doctor, I came about this pain. I'm just over my period and I couldn't go to work for three days. The only relief I was able to get was using a hot-water bottle and a fistful of Panadol.'

'Don't exceed the dosage,' he says suddenly. 'Panadol is dangerous enough.'

'Don't worry. I'm not a fool.'

'I can see that.'

She hears shuffling in the corridor outside. A knock at the surgery door.

'Excuse me a minute.'

The doctor gets up and half-opens the door. 'I'll be a bit longer Mr O'Leary.'

'No, doctor. I'm only looking for the prescription. That's all I'm after.'

'The prescription?'

'You know. For herself. The usual.'

'But I put repeat on that Mr O'Leary. She can just take it in again. They'll fill it out a second time.'

'Is that a fact? Well now. Well, she's a lot better doctor.'

'Good good.'

'She doesn't be wandering around so much.'

'Good good. Mr O'Leary I'm with a patient.'

She hears his muttered goodbyes and his steps hesitating on the stairs. The doctor sits down again, the office chair creaking under his weight. Sandy sees that his belly bulges over the belt of his trousers, that the buttons are under pressure, the gap between spread by it. There is a suggestion of breasts further up, a slight bulge in the material on the left side of his chest. He has a biro and a thermometer in the shirt pocket.

'The thing is, don't mind me asking now and you don't have to answer, but I feel I have to ask. It wasn't a rape anyway was it?'

She bites down the anger. He is only doing his job. She would be the first to protest if doctors didn't ask these questions.

'No doctor,' she says. 'It isn't rape.' She takes a deep breath. Why should she care? She remembers the portrait of Padre Pio in the waiting room. This man could be a devout Catholic.

'My lover is a bit aggressive. He is . . . very forceful.'

'I see. And the neck and cheek?'

'I said it's none of your business. None at all.' She begins to get up.

'Sit down please, Miss Muldoon.'

'I like it hard,' she says savagely. 'I like it hard – is that all right? I like the things he does. It has fuck all to do with the pain. And neither has my fucking father anything to do with it. You're all the same you bastards. You think it's mental don't you? You think it's all in the fucking mind. Well it isn't. If I drop dead of cancer or something, let it be on your conscience!'

He is on his feet, his left hand outstretched plaintively. 'Please. Now there's no need for this. Please sit down.'

'You haven't a clue have you?'

'It may not be psychosomatic. I agree with you. We should investigate further.'

'You just like pawing me.' He is shocked. His mouth opens and closes twice. He steps backwards, colliding with the office chair, reaches down with his right hand and catches the chair-back.

'You're all the same,' she says.

'How dare you,' he says. 'I resent that.'

'Look, fuck off. Just fuck off.'

'Get out of my surgery.'

'I'm going.'

'I never heard such a thing.'

'Really?' she said, her hand on the door. 'Well imagine that!' She steps out into the corridor and swings the door shut behind her. She stumbles towards the staircase and takes the first few steps two at a time, jarring into each step, fighting a feeling of pitching outwards and downwards. She comes up hard against the banister where the stairs turns to the right. She thinks she cannot breathe properly, that the air is suddenly thick and unmanageable. She sees the glass door ahead of her, on the ground floor. Beyond that is the street, rush-hour traffic bumper to bumper.

Chapter Nine

'I was passing,' he said. On his way west. 'I knew your
sister Sheila very well. You might remember, I was at her
funeral.' I remembered all right. He came with a girl and
Mick Delany. That was centuries ago. 'What are you
doing with yourself now?' He could see if he looked
close enough. The blue pinafore of a Mercy girl. 'I'm
doing my Leaving,' I said. 'Hard work so,' he said. I said
that it was brutal. I smiled knowingly, a grown-up girl
now, trying to suggest maturity. I was any simpering
child in the presence of an adult. What was he? Ten years
older than me? Fifteen? Not that big a jump. 'Is it the
Mercy?' I nodded. A Mercy girl. It was like those women
who sell cosmetics, door-to-door saleswomen, the Avon
Lady. A Mercy Convent girl was something specific.
Then he said he'd better be going and I said he should
come in and meet my mother. He said he would so, if he
wasn't intruding. He got out of the van and pointed to
the name. Micro Solutions. 'That's me,' he said. 'That's
what I'm doing now.'

'Do you remember the fellow you came with that

time? The time of the funeral. Delany the hurler?' In the background voices on the radio news were talking about Charlie Haughey's options. It was a hung Dáil, but Haughey would be Taoiseach. The only question was with whom would he do the deal.

'Mick?'

'How is he getting on?'

'He's married now. He married the girl who was with us. Nora.'

Anyway, my thoughts had turned elsewhere by then. They had become more specific.

Mammy was delighted to meet him. She shook his hand several times. I'm delighted to meet you. Delighted to meet you. Poor Sheila. The whole sorry mess related again. Daddy warned her not to go. But she was mad for the road. But there was snow forecast and black ice by all accounts. The priest was first on the scene. Wasn't it a miracle. Our own PP. The poor man was in tears telling us. But he gave her absolution. And weren't ye very good to come all the way for the funeral. And poor Daddy. Didn't he take bad afterwards. It destroyed him. It did.

It was the family fable, the great affliction. Funny the way things turn out after all. One big happy family and then. That's life. God's will I suppose. Though I can't understand it. No I can't understand it at all at all. Time heals all. Poor Sheila. Poor Daddy.

Then the conversation turned to me. How great I am at the books. First in my class in the convent though there was a bad spell there a while back. A reaction I suppose. But she's settled down to the books now. Father Bennis very proud of me. The whole family proud. All the boys gone now and the farm let out in conacre. The Bronx. Sure, half the hurling team is in the Bronx. They all meet up regularly someplace. And Alice wants to go to college herself.

What do you want Alice? *It's our secret.*

That was the first question. Open ended. What did I want?

I walked home from the bus now. Three miles. Sometimes he passed on his way to a meeting or to visit people. He blew his horn merrily. Waved his hand. He wore sunglasses. You could not see his eyes behind the mirrors. I heard that he visits another house. I won't mention names. I went to mass but I never went to communion. I had learned not to take what his hands offered. It was hard-won knowledge. It is two years since my last confession. Bless me father. The benison of Father Bennis.

'Escape.'

My mother laughed. 'Will you listen to her! Is it in prison you are.'

I was betrayed I realised. I covered up. I felt heat varnish my cheeks. 'I mean I want to get away from school,' I said, but I knew he saw through it. 'I'm sick and tired of the nuns. I want to go to college.' I thought suddenly of the wet road stretching ahead, the gleam of sunlight, a low winter sun polishing the future to shining steel. Sweet Jesus take me away before I am poisoned. Two years before the stream that follows the road below the house was polluted, run-off from a farmyard silage pit. The farmer said it was a teaspoonful, that he didn't think it would be so bad. No one believed him. In April Chernobyl burned, a country emptied and its children died or were consumed. But children are consumed all over the world, their bodies and their souls, here as well as there. And I knew that an atom is enough. The tiny seed of calamity propagates and colonises. A swelling bloom in the surface, and the gleaming fish float belly-up, obscene, putrefying; the children age and grow wary, pollution crackling in their distorted souls. I knew that my end would be the same.

Mammy shook her head and smiled. 'The young

ones these days Mr Lynch. They always want something else. It's always this or that. Something new all the time. When I was her age I was lucky to have a ribbon to my hair or shoes to my feet. They were the hard times I tell you.'

The ritual of tea. The kettle sang on the range. Winter or summer that range warmed the house. Sometimes it was so hot I had to open all the windows. A ghost of wind was welcome. The teapot was scalded, mother swishing water round and round, talking all the time about childhood, the glories of it, the little sufferings, the falls, the cracked knees, the bee-stings of innocence. The box was taken down. One spoonful for each and one for the pot. 'One spoon for us and one for the pot.' Fog filled the air. Clothes felt damp. The kettle was lifted screaming and the water swashed into the pot. The fog settled. The kettle was shifted sideways. The pot was never stirred. Cups clattered from the cupboard, saucers because we had a visitor. A cup in the hand? A sup of tea? You'll have a bite of something? Biscuits. Marietta. Chocolate Goldgrain. 'Now Mr Lynch. Have a wet of that.' The brown splashed into the white. 'Milk and sugar?' The tea party. Daddy's transistor radio hissed faintly about Terry Waite kidnapped in Beirut. That was his evening ritual, 'What's going on in the world at all?' The radio became his voice, his presence. Death cannot silence the news.

'Computers, you said. Now we're hearing all about them. The coming thing, they say.'

'I never even saw one,' I said.

'Well there's a van-load of them outside the door. They're not a pretty sight.'

But then he began to talk: about artificial intelligence; experiments he had read about; new software that would allow ordinary people to use them; computers communicating with each other; banks and governments and the military all keeping track of ordinary people through databases. Computers designed to function like the human brain, learning from themselves, learning by mistakes.

'Lord save us Mr Lynch, where will it all end?'

'It won't end at all,' he replied. 'The only barriers are the size of a piece of wire or an atom even, and the limits of the human mind.'

I think he glowed when he spoke about machines, a kind of cold glow like the new blue light the butcher had over his meat to kill insects.

'Someday we'll all have one. There'll be no more money, no books, no people in shops. Everything will be computerised.'

He was part of this extraordinary future, I realised. Part of the next age. I still lived in a community where there were occasional houses without electricity or running water. Where many farmers milked cows by hand. Where one man still ploughed with a horse because he hadn't enough land for a tractor. I saw his fashionable blazer, the broad colourful tie, the flared trousers.

'I'm going to Killarney,' he said. 'I have a bit of business down there. Will I take Alice for a run with me? I'll get her a bite to eat and drop her back about eleven.' Mother smiled. 'It'll do her good.'

'Exactly. Take her out of herself a bit. You said she was stuck in the books all day long. We could talk about university. Will you come for a spin, Alice? Down to Killarney?'

I shrugged. 'I don't mind.'

I have had a certain experience of cars. The last time I travelled in one. *A lift home. Lift that gymslip. Lift.* 'Well now child,' he said. 'You're getting big.'

I said nothing. Fuck the bastard.

'Will we pull over at the usual place?' I said nothing. 'My my we're in a sulk today. Did school go badly? Did you get lines? Bold girl.'

The sarcasm is heavy. Even at fourteen I can recognise it, the contempt in his voice, the tart superiority.

'I hear you're not doing a stroke. One of the worst messers in the class. Sister Benedict told me. She said you're forever getting lines. They tell me you were caught smoking in the toilets.'

I stared at the passing fields. My schoolbag on my lap. A small provision against his interest.

'Why won't you talk to me? You're a naughty child you know. You're going the high road to hell at the present moment. That's a fact. How long is it now? It must be three months since I heard your confession. And I'm keeping tabs on you like your poor dead father asked me. I know what's going on. I know everything. You were in the toilet with another girl. What were you doing with her?'

Smoking.

'If you know everything you needn't ask me.'

His nostrils flare when he is angry or excited. He held his head high like a horse whinnying. He shuffled his feet on the pedals.

'Saucy. Saucy. God in Heaven is looking down at you. And your father is watching over you. Do you know that? I know he's watching over you.'

He's making a poor job of it.

The road winds at the County boundary, stony outcrops and steep sided valleys. We talked about school and college. We talked about Sheila. 'You were her boyfriend,' I said. He nodded. 'I was. I was in love with her.'

'She was beautiful.'

'She was. Oh she was.'

'She was very like me.'

'The image of you.'

I was astonished at the naked desire in his face. Ten years since she died and it was still there. I know it. I know the carnal when I see it. The carnival of carnality. The merry-go-round of want, have, hate, hurt. The three-card-trick man finding the lady and losing her.

'Do you still miss her?'

He stared at the road, his hands joined across the top of the steering wheel, leaning slightly forward.

Everything in my life happens in cars.

'Not so much any more. Only when I think about her. I suppose I don't think about her much any more.'

'Did you ever find anybody else?'

'No.'

'Nobody?'

'I used to go out with that girl. Nora. The one that married Mick Delany.'

'Did he take her off you?'

'You're very direct.'

I have learned to be reckless. The consequences are not as bad as being safe. I remembered that it was Mick Delany I expected, Mick the Hurler, the hero, to come and carry me away, to pull hard and with a single blow to shatter the skull of Bennis the Bastard. I felt slightly betrayed. I felt hurt. I felt like hurting.

'He did in a way. But in another way, I was only covering up. Using her to cover things up. We were good friends really.'

'You slept with her.'

'Jesus Christ! What age are you?'

'I'm sixteen. Old enough to know.' I felt like Meryl Streep in *The French Lieutenant's Woman*. I knew things.

'To know what. Look it's none of your business.' But he told me anyway. He did. For a while. It started the night Sheila died. When he told me that he looked pained and angry at the same time. But I no longer wanted that. Pain is a curious thing. Once you have inflicted it the idea of it loses its potency. At least for me it did. It was a means to an end but the end was empty. 'I understand.' He slept with her the night Sheila died. It was a consolation. He buried his head in her and when he came out again the sand had shifted and the danger had gone. I could do it too. I could hide.

'When we lost Sheila,' I said, 'everything changed. I lost my sister and then my father died. I hardly know my mother now.' *I promised your poor father*. 'Sometimes I think I lost myself.' *Get a grip on yourself*. The image of someone skipping at the funeral, a girl skipping and counting, and Mick Delany the hurler who did not come back. That was Nora, skipping. 'So long Alice,' Nora said.

It's all over now child.

So long Alice.

'I'll comfort you,' he said. 'I can be your comfort. I can be your rock of safety. I know no one can ever know about us. But we can be together in secret. It'll be our secret.' He was at the pleading stage. It always started with anger, punishment, hell, the all-seeing eye. I was a bold girl. A wicked girl. A jezebel. A slut. A whore. A bitch. I had ruined his life. I had made him dishonour his vows. A double vow. The vow to God and the vow to my father. Then knowledge. That was his secret weapon. He had the advantage of me of course. He had tea at the convent and heard all the gossip. I take a personal interest in many of the girls, sister, because they are my parishioners. I like to keep an eye on things. And the nuns obliged. Knowledge is power. And he had the confessional. My friends thought he was a lovely man, an ideal confessor, shocked by nothing, a giver of light penances. They told him what they did with their boyfriends, how far they let them go, where they went: and he gave them three Hail Marys and three Our Fathers. He told them that what they were doing was natural but sinful. They must not feel ashamed telling him, but they must make a firm purpose of amendment. He hoped that next time he will hear a better confession from them.

Sometimes I was in their confessions. I smoked now. Someone told him that. I wrote his name on the inside door of the school toilets and underneath I wrote 'wanker'. He knew the following Monday. He said he was surprised that I knew such words.

'I know you have got yourself on the wrong road to spite me,' he said. 'But there's no need for that. I love you Alice. The way I loved your sister, with a pure and giving and a Christian love. If you put your trust in me I can comfort you.' *Though I walk in the valley of darkness thou art with me and thy rod and staff me comfort still.* I felt as if I was falling downwards off the edge of the earth, the world slipping by, objects going by so slowly that I could reach out and touch them, pick them up. I could take them with me but I knew if I did they would be changed, they would lose their shape, their purpose, and become monsters, sins, crudities. I reached out to claw for a hold and found flesh, an obscene planet. I held hard. I heard him cry out. I stopped. Surprised, I looked at him rubbing his face and I understood that I too could hurt. I deserved that. Even the Christians were given weapons, futile in the face of brute hunger, but representing some faint hope.

'Pride goes before a fall,' he said when I slammed the door. He wound down the passenger window and shouted: 'Mind that now my girl. Pride goes before a fall.'

He had a cassette player in the car with four speakers. This was my first taste of the encircling effect of music. The cab was warm although the instruments and packing cases in the back rattled and squeaked. Neil Young. 'I dreamed I saw the knights in armour coming.' There was a gale blowing up out of the west and we were pelting into it, the wipers going like crazy. I settled back and heard the magic words and felt the heat and thought about escape.

'Would you do it for me tonight Alice? Just one last time?' The car was stopped in the usual place. I knew where the handle was now. Although it was a Volkswagen Golf nowadays, the latest thing. A diesel engine. Austere and economical. Worthy of a man of God.

'No.'

Now the final phase. I felt my stomach muscles contract. Already there was pain. I knew if I did not concentrate I would soil myself. The humiliation would be unbearable, my sandwiches returning to the light of day in a long bubbling fart. This failure was for me the worst of all my body's failures: that here in the presence of my enemy I lost the most ordinary control, the control that had been taught by my mother from my earliest months. It was too much to bear, to focus on escape and control at once, to concentrate on the weaving and ducking of his words, the manipulation, and at the same time to exert a simple order on a single animal muscle. He had laughed at me the first time. Afterwards I had to explain to my mother that I had been taken short in the road and couldn't reach a gate in time. But when he bought the Golf he bought a set of removable covers. Like a wise virgin, always ready.

'I've been thinking of asking for a transfer.'

I nodded, concentrating on the squirming muscles, the cramp low down. He had been thinking of asking for a transfer for months, maybe years. Now I was old enough I wondered why it was diarrhoea and not vomiting that took me. Vomiting made more sense, a gargantuan spewing up of everything I held inside me. It seemed even my unconscious wanted to vitiate.

'They do that for us. The ones that get involved.' I remember thinking: he thinks he's involved. For him it's some kind of affair. His bishop probably sees it as an immoderate love, a lack of self-control. He fell in love with a girl. Sinned with her. Temptation is everywhere, Lord save us. There but for the Grace of God. We'll have to do something for the poor man. Get him out of this entanglement. 'I'd probably be sent to England for a while. I wouldn't mind that.' He smiled at me, genuinely happy at the thought. He was relaxed. 'They'd investigate the whole thing of course. That can't be helped. Someone from the Diocese would come down.' His hands rested on his stomach, his thumbs twirling contentedly. Below that I saw that his pants bulged. This was his foreplay.

We ate in the Wimpy. A mixed grill. Rashers, sausages, black and white pudding, a lamb chop, chips and peas. He asked me if I drank. I said I did. It was a lie.

He took me to a winebar and bought me a glass of wine and it filled my head. I was won over by the fake wine-barrels in the walls, the coloured bottle-ends in the glass, the suggestion of sawdust on the floor. He took money from a leather wallet and paid the barman with a flourish. Something studied, sophisticated. 'A dry white?' I nodded, not knowing whether dry was good or bad. We sat at a pine table and talked about a thousand things. The future was important to him.

'I'm going to make a million.' Until then I had not considered the future. His intentions were like a campaign, the expansionary dreams of an aristocrat: nothing I had seen before was ever like this. There were no small farmers with such dreams. No boys at discos who talked of thousands, never mind millions. Not one acre here would ever burst its banks and rumble over dry-stone walls to colonise a bog or make fertile the stony hills.

'Look,' he said. 'We've made a machine that can think. Not much yet. But that's only a matter of time. Each new machine will learn from the last. It's like Darwin's evolution. One of these days the world will be full of thinking machines. And the pace is incredible. I'm going to be there when it happens. I'm not going to spend the rest of my days servicing software. I have investments.'

I was afraid to invest, fearing the power of the mind to transform brute reality. But now I invested in him. It was half-conscious. I decided to place my future in him and hope for a return.

Afterwards we walked along the wet streets looking into shop windows and laughing at the leprechauns and shillelaghs. He stopped by a jeweller's window and said the next time he came he would buy me something. He pointed to a pair of silver earrings, serpents coiled and self-consuming. Celtic Gems, the cardboard said, Traditional Irish Craft. For the first time since childhood I lusted for an object.

I was sixteen. Who could blame me?

When it started to rain I stood into a deeper doorway and he followed me in. There in the darkness I kissed him. It was a thing I had not done before, although I understood the theory. Father Bennis had discussed it in detail with me but refrained from it himself. I think he thought it too personal.

I kissed him with rage. My lips crushed him. I poured my pain and anger into his mouth, sucking the darkness up and spitting it into him. When his tongue showed me the way I stuffed it in. I held nothing back. After that I knew where I was going.

Amor vincit omnia was the motto of the nun in *The Canterbury Tales*. Our teacher told us it was a joke, a quotation from Ovid or some other lewd writer. Not appropriate to nuns. The irony not to be explained to Mercy girls. But it was what we all thought. Love conquers all. If only we could have recognised it. For the crippled, the wounded, the sick, love was an impossible thing, a thing to be seized should it appear, never to be released. The crippled love with such intensity that it is years, perhaps a lifetime, before they come to see the beloved. And I loved Paddy, I think. Who knows why or how. I loved him because he would rescue me from crippledom, but also because he was the opposite of everything I was surrounded by. His armour gleamed in the wintry sun, in the imagination of sixteen years. His lance was poised to transfix the dragons of my nightmare. I was not to know he was the false knight.

It was always one last time. But I noticed that the times were stretching out. Weeks would go by. I understood that he had found another source. His black cloud had enveloped something else. It was raining in someone else's life.

I speculated as I held him. Who was it this time? She would be ten or eleven years of age. Twelve at the most. Weakened by suffering. I could think of two. One was crippled by arthritis of the childhood kind, her knuckles swollen, her legs crooked. She was in pain most of the time, her hair thinned and dead looking. She had big warm eyes. Trusting eyes. If he could put aside her physical imperfection, he might choose her. But her disease might make the act itself unpleasant. Another had an alcoholic father who beat her, her brothers and her mother. She had the grey look of the habitually terrified. Sometimes she did not go home at night but stayed with a neighbour. When her mother had a black eye or a bruise she said she was forever falling, that there was something wrong with her balance, her inner ear. The doctor was mystified by it, she said. She had learned the creativity of simple lies. She told her schoolfriends that her uncle in America was a test pilot with the Air Force. He was coming home to adopt her. She might as well say she was going to marry the Prince of Wales.

We are entitled to dreams. Even the crippled can dream of wholeness, the lame of walking, the prisoner dreams of the wind in his face. I make no apology for my dreams, the shadowland where all is made right, fortune is reversed and there are endings and beginnings. I say love can begin there. Paddy was my beginning. I thought he was glamorous and successful and I would escape with him, leave Bennis and the farm and the neighbours and the girls in my class. No more smoking in the toilets and scrawling graffiti. No more hatred eating the heart and burning the eyes. We drove home without looking at each other. It wasn't until we were a mile from the farm that he pulled in. I was hurt by his silence, ready to scratch and tear. He left the engine running, the heat on full, the wipers swashing water out of the light.

'We have to talk,' he said. *Don't talk child. Our secret.*
'We must.'
'I don't know what to say.'
'You're shocked.'

'Surprised.'

'I have had other boyfriends you know. Just because I'm a convent girl doesn't mean I'm naïve.' I was aware of the word 'naïve', falling at the end of the sentence that might have ended on so many other words. I was proud of it. A surprise. *Surprise surprise. It's not so hard now is it?* There never was a boyfriend, no slow beginnings, and Father Bennis was not a subtle man in the end. And though I had not been an innocent for many a year, and I knew the way, still I knew nothing worth knowing. Paddy was my only hope.

'I never thought you were naïve. I just thought you were . . . Look. I like you. I'd like to see you again.'

'The same again please.' I said it the way he had ordered my second glass of wine in the bar in Killarney. It was brutal.

'I don't deserve that.'

'No,' I said. 'I suppose you don't. It wasn't what I meant to say.' *That's the right way to do it. Your hand there. The finger – I'll show you.*

'We're in the 1980s.'

'Don't I know.'

He put his arm around my shoulders and looked me in the eye. 'But you know how I felt about Sheila,' he said. I was an expert in secrets and yet I never detected his. I heard the words only. The truth about Sheila was encrypted there, about his love. I had no key and the deciphering has taken years: in the end only chance would make me see it for what it was.

'The way I said I felt. You understand?'

His arm was warm, his fingers played lightly on my shoulder. I remembered a skipping song that Sheila used to sing: I'll buy you a paper of pins, cause that's the way that love begins, if you'll marry, marry, marry, if you'll marry me.

And I thought: this is the way that love begins.

'You were her lover,' I said. 'Now you'll be mine. I think that's nice.'

Then he was grateful. Promising me everything. He would look after me. He would make sure I got on well at the Leaving. He would make the way smooth at university. He wouldn't say a word to my mother.

He buttoned himself up and pulled out into the road again. I turned on the radio. It was all right this time. I suppose, the more you do things the more you become exempt from what they mean. At least, that is the way things should go. As opposed to that there are certain things that are impossible. It is impossible that a little girl should lose her self to a priest. That all the joy should be stolen. All the years of dreaming of boys, the fussing with clothes and hair, the plans, the secret letters, the whispers between friends, the naming of names, the night before the disco and the next day. Instead there is no mystery. The great gap of dreams is filled with a dead weight of unwanted knowledge. The magnitude of that knowledge is a number too large to be computed.

Mammy was waiting at the door. I think she was becoming suspicious. So late at night, almost one o'clock. She looked at him and I could see she was trying to penetrate those eyes. I know she did not succeed because when I did tell her it broke her heart. 'Why didn't you say something,' she screamed. 'I could have stopped it.' It was the only time in my life that I heard her scream. It was like a physical pain. I still hear it.

'You should have told me,' she says. 'You could have phoned from Killarney. I was terrified. I was sure you were after going in over the ditch down the County bounds. I was picturing the car down in the valley in the rain.'

She was thinking of Sheila of course. One fatal crash is enough in any family.

I should have told her. Then everything would have been all right. If only I could have opened to someone I might never have fallen down. This place. Where I have fallen. But at least I did not fall alone. We fell together. I could forgive him if he knew less. Or knew more. He has never asked me where I learned those things. In a way it doesn't matter to him. In the beginning he just wanted them. A kind of perverse simplicity made me give them to him. Then he came to depend on me. It eased his burden, he said. The stress of his position was unbearable. His trips to the farm were the only thing that kept him going. In his job everything was in the open, no secrets, no hidden corners. I was his counterweight, a rock balanced on the edge, something he could hide under and fear at the same time.

'Aaah,' they say. They ease themselves. That is the way it goes. In the end we are intermediaries. They name parts of engines after us: the female receives the interlocking male, a place for insertions, a receptor. And they spray their seed into the night air with the same satisfaction as into our taut interior. The dynamic itself is wasteful, an outpouring. No one waits eagerly for a sup, no infant at breast is hungering for it. It has no useful purpose for them. A waste. Seed spoiled. Their brief suffering flows out of them, polluting all it touches.

She was fixing my veil in front of the big mirror in her bedroom, bubbling with joy. I lost my mother when I lost my sister – her grief swallowing her love. She nursed my father and grieved for Sheila and in the current between those two cold continents I drifted into the priest's net. Where did my childhood go? Under a lorry one dark night? Or into a warm car? I lost it in the folds of Father Bennis's black suit. Mother, I could have told you, should have told you. But I thought you would not listen. I believed I was alone. Now she thinks my marriage is made in Heaven, the man who came to pay his last respects to my sister falling in love with me. It was God brought us together, Daddy guiding it from above. 'God bless you child,' she said, 'but you look radiant. Radiant.'

'Thank you,' I said.

'I only wish you were getting married at home. Father Bennis would be so happy. He always had a soft spot for you. He's so proud of you, you know.' Happy Father Bennis performing the nuptials, looking forward to the bit of grub, the music. Happy for the young people.

'Paddy wanted to get married in the city. For business reasons.' I looked at her face in the mirror and saw that it was my own thirty years from now. The emptiness terrified me. The future was irredeemable. There was no turning back.

'Business business,' she said. 'You'll have to mind that man or he'll work himself to death. You'll have to make him take holidays. You should book a holiday in Majorca or someplace every year. That way he can't get out of it.'

'I will Mammy.'

'Fancy him falling for you on that spin to Killarney. I'll pin back this bit or else it'll keep falling into your eyes.'

'It was the other way around Mammy,' I said. 'I made him fall for me.'

'Sure of course you did child. You fell for him first.'

'I did it to get away.'

Her mouth bristled with pins. She had to put three into my veil before she could speak. 'What's that you're saying?' She said it abstractedly. It was a tangent, a meaningless interpolation, almost garbled by the pins.

'To escape?'

'Whisht child. What are you saying?' She leaned back against the end of the bed. She looked puzzled. She eased her lips into her palm and the pins fell out, a litter of steel shavings winking in the light.

Then I thought of her standing in the bright doorway as I left the car, the slow walk towards her as he pulled out. Where were you until now? Were you with Father Bennis all this time? What do ye have to be talking about?

You put me in his hands, I thought. You gave me over to him. You gave up when Daddy died, glad that someone loved me. Do not think that you are free from guilt. He'll pick you up after school. Take you home. Nice Father Bennis takes a personal interest in my daughter. One or two other daughters also. One of them died the other day. In tragic circumstances. Did you know that Mammy? One of them jumped off a bridge in Cork. Her pockets were full of stones. Bulges in her denims, in her tartan jacket. She jumped off a bridge and Father Bennis said her funeral mass. How do I know she was one of his? Because we all know each other, that's the truth. We see it in each other's faces. We are a club. We meet in the girls' toilets in the Convent of Mercy and we pretend that we are there to smoke and play cards. We talk about boys. Oh, there are some who never talk at all. Or smoke. Some who never put a foot wrong. I can only guess about them.

'I want to love him. But I don't. I want to love *someone*.'

She put her hand to her mouth. Her eyes are wide.

This is the worst thing that has happened to her since Sheila died. Possibly worse. Pins rain on her cardigan, her skirt, the carpet. Gleaming.

'What are you saying?'

'I said I don't love him. I'm only marrying him to get away.'

She walked away from me. She went to the door but didn't open it. Then she turned round and walked back. She slapped me in the face.

'How dare you,' she said.

I thought: she thinks I want to escape from her.

'I don't think I'm able to love anyone,' I said. 'I'm sorry.'

'Sorry? Sorry for what? That's what I want to know. What did you do? What have you to be sorry about?'

'I'm sorry I'm marrying him.'

'Don't so.' It was snapped out, hard, hurt.

'I have to escape.' I could see her hand clenching. 'Not from you,' I almost shouted. 'Not you Mammy.'

'Who so?' She was shouting now. 'Who so?'

'Oh God,' I said. 'I can't say it. I never said it to anyone.'

'Sweet suffering Jesus, WILL YOU SAY WHAT'S ON YOUR MIND!'

I remember stumbling backwards. I fell against the wall near the spindle-legs of the dressing-table. I remember the rattling of the coloured bottles of scent she kept on it. Then I slid down to the ground and doubled my knees up. The veil came down over my face. I remember thinking that the carpet would dirty the wedding dress. I would never get it clean for tomorrow.

'I hate him. I hate him,' I said. I was crying. It was the first time I had cried in three years. 'All of them. I hate all of them.'

'Who are you talking about child?' Her composure was back. My mother was the most composed person I ever met. She took everything in her stride. She managed my father with skill. She ran his funeral like a campaign, managed us and the house and the farm. She was a cool one.

So I told her and she screamed. It was as if she knew. When I mentioned his name she screamed. It was enough, but I went on, the filth spilling out of me, pent up over all the years, the sewer bursting its banks and pouring out, spoiling everything. She sat on the kitchen chair, straight-backed, silent, and I emptied her life of anything worthwhile. When I was finished she walked out and I never really spoke to her again. She died the following year. A stroke, swift and merciful. She did not know the ministrations of the church, the communion brought to her bedside, the visitations. Father Bennis gave her the last rites but she was probably already dead. What would he have made of her confession?

Chapter Ten

'But did you know her my dear?' Old Cleary is fussing as usual. 'Did you know the poor lady? Her husband is a customer you know. You must have met him a dozen times since you came to us.' There was no 'us', just Billy Cleary. Billy Cleary did the accounts, such as they were, typed, hung the pictures and occasionally served the wine. Galleria Clary. 'He's in insurance. He hardly ever buys but it's good for people like him to be seen here. Good for them and good for us. It raises the tone. When those kind of people meet each other they like to flash their chequebooks. Flash their chequebooks my dear. That's what it's all about. Come to think of it, he did buy a picture once. A hideous object. Quite picturesque, you know the kind of thing. I'll tell you what. I'll give you a personality profile of people like our Mr Delany. And this applies to any Mr Delany you'd care to name. I except the two percenters.' The two percenters are that segment of society that Billy Cleary said had *some* culture. Not a lot. Some. 'Let me see. Stopped reading at fourteen. Stopped going to the cinema at eighteen.

Stopped listening to music at twenty-one. Married at twenty-four. Stopped playing games, team games anyway, at twenty-five. Comes home in the evening and plonks, plonks down in front of the telly. Buys his art in Tesco and brings it home in a plastic bag.' He ends triumphantly, a sly grin on his face. 'Am I right or am I wrong?'

She laughs. 'You're right Mr Cleary. As always.'

He is delighted. 'That's only one small smidgen from my bag of tricks. I'm a riot at parties. For instance I can tell the kind of cars people drive by looking at their lipstick and hair. I may tell you Sandy, I know quite a lot about lipstick and hair. I'm almost a connoisseur.'

'Do you often go to parties?'

'Only interesting ones. Nowadays there are very few interesting ones anywhere in the world. I am well-informed about that too. I have my network. I can pick up the phone and call say, Rhode Island, and say "Anything good going down over there?" I will get the low-down, straight from the horse's mouth. So to speak. Ballydehob – now there's a tricky one. But yes, you've guessed it, the network extends even that far.'

'Turn left at the next, Mr Cleary.'

'Left-hand turn coming up my dear.' He shifts down to second and the car screeches and bumps, slows, revs loudly and takes the left-hand turn in low spirits. 'As a matter of fact your old friend Tim Bredin has been making indiscreet enquiries about you. Did I tell you that? I heard it last week. I've been keeping it under my hat.' He lifts the chequered peaked cap he is wearing. 'Behold. Indiscreet enquiries. I may say his lust is palpable. Or would be if I could get close enough to palpate it. I think he set his sights on you at the opening of his exhibition, but of course, his mind was elsewhere at the time. Cupidity is his speciality my dear. Nothing must come between Tim Bredin and a sale. Not friend. Not wife. Not mistress. Not God. Definitely, God would be in the wrong place if he came between Bredin and a sale.'

'Left again.'

'We're going round in circles. Or at least squares. Rectangles rather.'

'No there's a right second next. We'll be there then.'

'I love funerals. They remind me of life. I never feel so spry as when I've just seen someone off. Weddings have the opposite effect. At weddings I become melancholy and muse about death and the afterlife. I must say, the afterlife doesn't sound inspiring. From what we hear about it, the network won't function there. I think, whatever else may be said for the place, we may safely assume that the network would be out of kilter.'

'They say there's a place for everyone.'

'Not for buggers my dear. God has always had a down on buggers.' Sandy laughs outright. 'You find the term amusing? You would prefer gay?' He shakes his head sadly. 'The word "gay" to my generation means happy. To say you are gay means to say you are happy. Even buggers can't be happy all the time. Besides, "gay" is a state of mind. Buggery is an activity. A delightful activity. It is like saying someone is a footballer. One is defined by one's predilections. A tradesman, for example, would pride himself on his trade. If I were a plumber . . .' He pauses, then breaks into song, 'If I were a carpenter and you were a lady, would you marry me anyway? would you have my baby?"

'Oh Mr Cleary,' Sandy says, eyes sparkling, 'I thought you'd never ask.'

His laughter quickly becomes a fit of coughing. When he recovers he says, 'I like you Sandy. Not just because you're good for business. Although, God knows, having Bredin chasing your tail is sure to bring him back. No I'm fond of you because you're like me.'

'How am I like you. That's it. Just ahead.'

'Look at that bastard. People forget they have indicators.' The car screeches to a halt while a Hiace van pulls out into the traffic and speeds away. Then he parks the car laboriously, his tongue protruding from between his teeth like a child with a problem in sums.

'As I was saying, you're like me in a way. Nothing much matters to you. You're fun-loving, that's what you are. I'm a fun-lover too. We make a good pair.'

'Thank you. I take it as a compliment.'

'And well you may. But let me tell you this, the game you are playing is a dangerous one.'

'What game?'

'You know very well what I'm saying. Sandy, be careful. Alice Lynch is a dangerous woman. Don't provoke her.'

Sandy is suddenly reserved, her face a blank. 'I don't know what you're talking about. I know nothing about Alice Lynch.'

'Ah my dear, but I do. The network you know. She's cold. Cold cold cold. Through and through. You may think she's a warm, happy creature, a thing of airs and graces. A typical rich woman with a fast car and a liking for expensive pictures. Nothing between the ears perhaps. The network says otherwise. I wouldn't like to see you hurt. Look, isn't that the blushing widower?'

Mick Delany has arrived. With his arrival the machinery begins to move. The hearse door swings upwards. The po-faced undertakers step forward, hands joined low down in front like footballers awaiting a free kick. The mourners form a discreet line. Behind them Sandy recognises the doctor. Out of his surgery now he looks a bigger man, more assured, less reptilian. He has a slight stoop which doesn't show when he is seated in his surgery chair. It makes him look thoughtful, paternal, caring.

'John, what brings you here?' He is standing at the back in a fawn-coloured duffel-coat. He says that he's a friend of a friend. Anyway, he read about it in the newspapers. A strange case. But his eyes are drawn, his skin pale.

'Are you all right Johnny?'

'I'm not sleeping that's all. The last two nights. Too much study I suppose. Burning the candle at both ends.'

'You look shagged. You should take it easy.' She knows he is studious, one of those rarely seen wasting hours in the student bar. She is a socialiser, even before the gallery job, a party-goer. Yet she still made her firsts, cramming in the short-term, aware of her own ability. She pities those like John who have to work.

'I was thinking about her,' he says, 'last night. And I came across something that seemed to be true. I think it was the connection. Between reading about the suicide and then finding this thing in Kierkegaard. I think that was a kind of fate. Something like that. I don't believe in fate as such of course.'

'Of course.'

'So I decided I'd go to the funeral.'

'What was the piece from what's his name?'

'I have it here. Look I wrote it down.' He pulls an envelope from his pocket and opens it. Inside is a piece of grey paper on which he had written: 'What if everything in life were a misunderstanding, what if laughter were really tears?'

'That's beautiful Johnny,' she says. 'Why have you it in an envelope?'

He blushes. 'I just have.'

'You're not going to put it in the grave or anything? Oh my God. Johnny don't do that.'

'I'm not,' he says sharply. He almost turns away from her, takes one step then stops, canted away a little, half-departed. He stands like that, a stiff statue, staring towards the gate. 'I never knew her,' he says. 'Why should I put anything into her grave for Christ's sake?'

'It's for someone so, isn't it? Go on, Johnny. You can tell me.'

John gazes steadfastly at the coffin.

'Go on, John,' she says softly. 'I don't mind any more. There's someone else in my life now.'

'Look. Over there. I can't point because it will be obvious. Standing at the back, behind the mourners.'

'The Lynchs?' The shock in her voice is obvious even to him.

'You know them?'

She covers quickly. 'They come to the gallery. Remember? I saw you discussing a painting with her but you never looked at her. Oh my God! Is it her? Was that what all that was about?'

He looks pained. 'That's her.'

'We have something in common so after all,' she says coldly.

'What?' But the prayers are beginning. They are expected to listen or reply, not talk to each other. In the gap between two decades of the rosary Sandy whispers, 'The last time we were all together was at the gallery.' When the prayers stop Sandy has moved on.

'I'm so sorry Mick,' Alice Lynch is saying. Her hand lingers in his and she looks up into his face, searching for sorrow or pain or some other symptom of his loss. She finds nothing, a clear grey eye, a still mouth, a steady hand.

'I should have known it was coming,' he says.

'You couldn't have stopped her,' she tells him. 'You can't stop people who want to do it.' But she knows immediately that she has said the wrong thing, that he had never considered stopping her. Not this time. The previous time they had still a life together, a relationship.

Now, for several years they were acquaintances, unpleasant neighbours. Little more.

'I loved her,' he says. 'Once.'

'You did Mick,' she tells him.

'But that's the way things go, isn't it? You never know what way your life will turn out. There was always a want in her. But I thought it was just fun. Do you remember I used to call her Crazy Nora? She was always mad for the crack. Always game.'

Someone else is standing at her shoulder. She moves on, shaking someone else's hand, a stranger in mourning. From behind she hears, 'I'm sorry for your trouble Mr Delany.'

It is the little thing from the gallery. Nice of her to come. Doctor Hennessy behind her. Wearing his funeral clothes.

Later they find themselves standing side by side.

'I feel I know you,' the little thing says.

'Really.' Alice knows how to be frigid with people like that. *You're a frigid bit. Do you know what frigid is? Frigid is sitting there and not making a sound. Say something. Oh for God's sake say something. I'm not going to eat you you know. I'm not a monster. You're so fecking silent.*

'Yes. I've watched you so much in the gallery.'

'Really?' There is a note of interest in Alice's voice.

'Yes. You've bought more pieces than anyone else on our list. I think you can know a person through their taste in art. A person's taste says a lot about them. I think I know you quite well.'

'I doubt it.' *They all know me. Sure none of them would believe a word you'd say.*

'I could be wrong.'

'I'm not that easy to know.'

'Does it make you uneasy? The thought of someone watching you? Studying your moves, the way you examine a picture or a sculpture, the way you stand back, lean your chin on your left wrist. That's the sign I love. That means you are affected. I've only seen it a few times. Maybe three. You stand back and lean your chin on your wrist. It's like the way some people bite their nails when they're excited. It's typical.'

'You have been paying attention.' *Listen to this. I'll explain all about sin to you.*

'It's my job. I sell it. You buy it. That's my life.'

'Hello Alice.' Doctor Hennessy. Then turning to Sandy. 'Well, hello.' He drifts on, making some remark about the weather as he goes. Alice turns a cold countenance on Sandy.

'You must excuse me. There's someone I want to see before I go. It's been interesting talking to you. No doubt we'll meet again.'

'At the gallery. Yes.'

'Yes. But also other places.'

'Don't laugh at me. What I said. I know more about you than you think.'

'I beg your pardon?'

But Sandy has turned away and is moving towards the gate, as are most of the other mourners.

'What are you doing here?' Alice stands in front of him, hands on her hips like a fishwife.

John wears his usual thin fawn duffel-coat, off-white trainers, blue denims. 'Came to pay my respects.'

'Bullshit. You didn't know her.'

'How would you know. Anyway I know you. And you know her. I feel connected.' And, he thinks, if I had accepted her invitation she might not be dead now, but no one has the right to accept the burden of another's death.

'If he sees you—'

'He's busy.' He jerks his thumb in the direction of a knot of men.

She sees Paddy in their midst, his back to her. *Father Bennis bulging in his black trousers, his ass stretching the seams, his chasuble on his arm, a missal in the other. Three priests, chatting and laughing. Looking forward to the bite of grub. Beyond that, the gravediggers waiting with shovels to fill the ground in over him.*

'I told you—'

'I know. You only want to see me in bed. Once you're satisfied you're gone again.'

She is stung. 'Walk down along with me,' she says. 'I'm sorry. I'm upset. I suppose I'm upset by Nora dying.'

Now it is his turn. 'Bullshit. You said she was a lunatic.'

'Well. I was right.' Nora overdosing in a cowshed. That was lunacy certainly. If Alice were to take an overdose it would be somewhat more elegant. And she is not the dying kind. She supposed she had survived more than Nora, gone to school to suffering from an earlier age. Nora was a loser.

They are moving among the gravestones, fuzzy lichen everywhere. Old dates, weird angels, pseudo-Celtic crosses, mock-heroic tombs, stones as thin as playing-cards. The dearly beloveds and the deeply regretteds. Spider-web cracks, fault lines in marble, the veins and arteries of the earth's birth. Death leaves her cold. These worthies sleep the sleep of the just, blessed by a church that is possessed by the spirit of Bennis.

'I suppose you were proved right by events. That's the ultimate proof for a rational being.'

'You'll have to give up philosophy,' she replies. 'It's making you ponderous.'

'I always was. It's not new. I brought you this.' He passes her the envelope.

'For God's sake John. Not here.' Then smiling and glancing over her shoulder. 'People will think you're selling me drugs.'

'You never came to the party.'

'I'm not a party kind of girl. Paddy is the party person.'

'Read what it says.'

She reads, her lips spelling out the words as though she had trouble reading. Then she slips the paper back into the envelope and puts it in her pocket.

'That's sweet,' she says.

'It's Søren Kierkegaard,' he tells her. 'It's from a book about choices.'

'I suppose that's intended to be meaningful.'

'You have to make a choice.'

They are out on the road now, approaching the knot of mourners that had gathered on a wider part of the path.

'I have made a choice,' she snaps. 'I always make choices.'

He is desperate. 'Meet me.'

She clucks in irritation then seems to regret it. She swings away so that her back is to him. In the distance cars are starting. The hearse is already gliding silently away. 'The picnic site at eight thirty so.'

'Goodbye.'

'Thank you for coming,' she calls after him. 'On behalf of Mick.'

'So that's the story,' Paddy says. 'We'll be announcing it next week Mick. It's top secret now of course, but I thought you might like to be in. We're letting selected people know in advance. Give them a chance to pick up a bit of stock. I know it's not the time or the place, but, well, for old time's sake I thought I'd let you know.'

'No no. Thanks very much. I appreciate the tip. You know the way it was with Nora and me. I probably have my head more straight today than I had this many a year.'

'She was a grand girl in her time,' Paddy says. 'A beauty.'

Doctor Hennessy says that she was a wonderful person. 'I was shocked when I heard,' he says. 'Shocked. But did you have any idea, Mick, any idea at all? I mean all those drugs. I never prescribed the half of them.' Mick shakes his head. 'It's true what they say,' the doctor says. 'The closest is always the last to know. And as Paddy says, she was such a beauty. I remember her the first time she came to me, the time of the miscarriage. I often think, if things were different – you know what I mean.'

'I do. I never figured out what came over her. Maybe it was me. She shouldn't have married me. Paddy, do you remember the night years ago coming home from the funeral? I said I was going to play for the County. The fact was she never believed me. She always thought I was going to do something else. She couldn't believe anyone could have their whole future mapped out before them the way I had. What really drove her mad was that it worked out exactly the way I said it. That got to her. It was like she was trapped in my plan. Trapped in my life I suppose.'

'Well,' Paddy says. 'You never know do you. You just have to do your bit.'

'That's the way.'

'How do you do it Paddy,' someone says. He is writing something on the back of his hand. 'Jaze you never put a foot wrong. No matter what, you always come out a few bob ahead. I have a few thou this time anyway. A few to spare for once.'

Paddy flashes a smile and holds up his hands. 'We do it with mirrors,' he says. 'Trust me. This one is good. They'll double in a week. You can take your profit and still have your stake. You can't lose.'

'Give me the name again,' the doctor says. 'Was it Micro Solutions?' He has his pen out, poised over the palm of his hand. 'I appreciate the tip I needn't tell you. Jaze, between retention tax and the bloody government—'

'How about a spot of shooting?' Paddy says. 'I have the gun back from Purdey's.' The doctor nods eagerly. 'A brace of duck,' he says. It sounds odd, out of tune.

Sandy Muldoon is making her way towards them. 'Hello,' she says. She looks at the doctor. He smiles a wan smile at her. 'Could I have a word with you, Mr Lynch. It's about the print your wife ordered.'

'Excuse me Mick.' Paddy walks her ten steps, his hand on her elbow. 'Don't fucking interrupt me in future. I'm doing business here. You're getting beyond yourself.' His fingers clamp her elbow and her arm goes suddenly limp. 'I'll see you later on. In the hotel.' He says it with a half-smile on his face so that everyone will think he is negotiating for a piece from the gallery. His voice is low, almost soft.

'Oh Jesus, go easy,' Sandy cries. 'Oh.'

The bed is slamming against the wall. The flimsy table that holds the bedside lamp is shaking.

'Shut up,' he tells her. 'Just shut fucking up.'

In a moment he says, 'Aaah' followed by a sound like 'Gnnnn'. Then he is quiet. She feels his dead weight relax on to her. After about half a minute he rolls sideways and she sees that his eyes are closed. She is furious. 'Is that all?'

'Shut up will you,' he whispers. 'You'll spoil everything.'

'You hurt me that time.'

'That time?'

'Yes. That time. You hurt me the last time too.'

'You like it.' He stretches and yawns.

'What?'

'You like being hurt. Or else you wouldn't come back for it.'

She rolls over on to her side and finds herself looking at the thin grey line of dust at the edge of the carpet that the Hoover could not catch. Here and there the fibres lick upwards from underneath, like insect legs trapped in the floor. And in fact there is the corpse of a woodlouse lying on its back in the corner like a miniature armadillo. She knows it would be as light as air if she moved it, hollow inside.

'Why did you pick me,' she says.

She swings her feet out and stands up. There is a long mirror at the end of the bed and she sees herself in it. There is blood on her thigh.

'Oh Jesus my period is after coming.'

'Fuck,' he says. He is up immediately searching for his underpants. 'Jesus Christ it's all blood.'

She stands up and looks down at him holding the blue underpants with the red gash in the middle of it. She starts to laugh. 'Your wife will think you had a sex-change!'

Afterwards she can't remember the movement that brought him up against her. She has an impression of speed, no more. But she remembers the blow, the solid thump as his hand hits her cheekbone. She remembers falling down, her shoulder hitting the bathroom door. She remembers that he kicked her in the legs, around the thighs first. When she rolls away and doubles up he kicks her underneath, a sickening pain. Then he is getting dressed calmly.

She remembers sitting up against the wall, her cheek throbbing. She is conscious of a dribble of menstrual blood on the carpet. He looks at her and she recognises his contempt.

'You asked for that,' he says. 'You dirty little bitch.'

She holds herself tight and doesn't cry.

'Don't be so dramatic John. I'm years older than you. You'll find there are plenty of other women who'll fall for your good looks.'

'Not like you.'

'Well there are plenty of boys like you.' She feels the abrupt contraction of regret. *You have to be cruel to be kind.* Was she becoming like him? Like Bennis? She is aware of the need to hurt, to punish. She thinks her being is slowly becoming his, a kind of piecemeal transubstantiation. They always get you in the end or the beginning, she thinks. Willing or not you become one of them. *You're in and you can't get out.*

'Not true,' he says, but he is wounded.

She almost laughs. Stops herself in time. 'You haven't got it in you, John, that's all. I need someone with a streak of cruelty.'

'I thought you didn't like that. Be gentle with me, remember? You said that to me the first night.' Lately he has been trying to piece together the fragmented memories of that night. It is a kind of piety, he thinks, a monument of memory. The trouble is he can only recall certain vivid moments. The first kiss. The moment he knew she would take her clothes off. Fumbling for the key to the front door. Waking up to the sound of a car horn blowing. They are like pieces of an intricate fretwork that had been pulled apart, each part depending on the next, so broken that the remnants could not be pieced together again.

'Kill him.'

'What?' Her face is suddenly bright, an open smile, her body loosening with a kind of joy. He stares at her, astonished by the transformation.

'That's what I said. Come to our house tonight. I'll leave a door open. We can break a window afterwards for the sake of form. No one will hear a thing. We're detached. We can't even hear our neighbour's lawnmower. Trees and a stone wall between.'

'Jesus! What are you talking about?'

'Come in through the open door. Go upstairs to our bedroom. Stab him or shoot him or hit him with an axe, I don't care. Chop his head off. When he's dead I'll give you the ride of your life.'

Alice is assailed by a crystal-sharp memory: she was standing in the parochial house, looking up the stairs, hopping from one foot to the other because she needed to go to the toilet. Father Bennis's housekeeper was glaring at her, her hands white with flour that had collected in drifts against the pockets of her apron. She could hear the creaking sound of the priest moving along the landing above. *I'm coming child.* 'My mother sent me. Mr Moloney isn't well at all.' Mr Moloney was dying in his damp lonely farmhouse a mile across the fields. *I'll give you a lift back child.* She wet herself in the car that night, fear draining down over the plastic covering, pooling on the grey carpet. His car smelled of piss for months afterwards. *I'll give you the ride of your life you little demon, he said. You wicked little sinful little bitch.*

'Jesus Christ I think you're serious.' He feels as if he were falling forward into a deep well, already drowning. He reaches out once to steady himself and finds the door handle unexpectedly. His instinct is to get out, to slip away, escape. He is thinking: The accused solicited a student to commit the murder.

'Do you believe in perfect love, Johnny?'

He gasps, seeing the trap. He will not walk in. And in the end it is no more than words. 'No. Not like they say. You know, the priest on the altar talking about Christ and perfection and everything. No I don't.'

'I mean perfect love between people.'

'That's just romantic novels.'

'I believe in it. Complete perfect love. Just like they

say in the sermons but with a bed thrown in. Nobody takes advantage of the other. Two people equally committed.'

'Equally compromised you mean. That's what you're saying, isn't it?'

'You have to prove it to me.'

'Not by killing him.'

'I'll live with you when it all dies down. We'll go away on a long holiday. A cruise maybe.' She sounds dreamy now, wistful, like a child planning a personal fairytale. 'In three years time I'll marry you and we'll be rich as well as everything else. Can't you see, I can't just leave Paddy. I can't just walk out. I'll lose everything. I have nothing, no life. I'm trapped.' There are knights who did such things, princes who slew ogres and stole girls from the grasp of the dragon. She thinks perhaps it was not too late. Somewhere inside of her there is still a small girl waiting to be kissed and transformed, a tiny sheltered creature, crouching in shadows. She senses the presence. There is more than one incubus. Come out Alice, she thinks. Now or never.

'Jesus.'

'I am serious.'

'I see you are. You're out of your mind.'

She shakes her head. She flicks on the lights and flicks them off again. The trees and picnic table jump in and out of focus, seeming to leap nearer in the light and vanish back into the darkness again. A car roars by on the road outside, lights screaming past among flickering ash trees and whitethorns.

'No,' he says. 'I couldn't do it.' He senses that she is smiling in the darkness and he is stung by it. 'If you are serious.'

'I am.' He can hear it in her voice. It is true. She wanted him to kill her husband. 'There's Nora Delany,' she says suddenly. 'The poor bitch. Stuck with that fat bastard all her life. A mistake. You can't undo a mistake but you can escape.'

'Why don't you just leave him? Why not just walk out?'

'I enjoy this,' she says carefully. Now her voice has a clean edge, her words enunciated rather than spoken, careful, directed. He sensed that she wanted to hurt him and sought in vain for a shield to guard against it. 'I don't remember many things about my childhood. But I remember once, a dog we had that got canker. My father said he had to be put down. It frightened me and made me sad. But I wanted to watch. Children are like that. I wanted to see what such a thing would be like. He wouldn't let me. He went out in the evening with the gun under one arm and the dog under the other. I told you I grew up on a small farm and that's the way things were done in those days. I heard the shot but I saw nothing. Instead I filled my imagination with pictures.' She stares at the windscreen, her eyes flicking from image to image as though she could see it all over again. Then she shivers and shakes her head. 'But I don't really love you, John. I don't love anybody as a matter of fact. I can't.'

'Except yourself.' It should be a return blow, not a parry. It fails, and he knows it. She has the control. He has lost any power he might have had. Still, her answer surprises him.

'Myself least of all,' she says. 'What I do is I hate people. It's not as much fun but it's a good substitute.' *Think of the worst torture you could imagine. That's hell for you. The worst thing that the Japanese did during the war. Only it goes on for ever. Do you know what infinity means?*

'This is going round in circles.' He catches her wrist and holds it fiercely, his fingers burning her skin. 'Are you serious?'

Yes. But the moment is lost. The future balances on

a knife-edge. Infinity lies between the instant of choice and the act. Between the going out at evening and the sound of the shot.

'No. I'm not. But I feel like it sometimes.'

She hears him sigh. He relaxes in the seat. 'You said you enjoy it. What do you enjoy? Just the sex?' That's the murder business out of the way, she thinks, now he can settle down to a good old row. A lovers' tiff, a quarrel, a falling-out. Some endless circling of the same congested district.

She loves me – she loves me not.

How much does she love me?

The juvenile form of the species has settled in. He does not live in the adult world, still thinks lives can be ordered by thought. A considered life. Authenticity. Too much philosophy.

But reality is a predator crawling all over them, devouring their substance, eating their lives from the inside out.

'You want me to say I enjoy sleeping with you.'

'Yes. If you do it's a start. It's the beginning of something. Or it *could be* the beginning of something.'

'Do you want the truth?' He nods, wary-eyed, watching her with care.

She is silent a moment.

'I enjoy fucking in cars. I enjoy the deception.' *I'll give you a lift home.*

'Shit.'

'The truth. I enjoy the betrayal too.'

He looks shocked. 'You're lying.' But he can sense the electricity in her. She is more animated than she has been since their first night together.

'I'd like him to find out. Paddy. I'd like him to find out about this. Except that I'm frightened.'

'Frightened? Why are you frightened?'

'Tie your pants up. I'm dropping you home.' *Fix*

your gymslip. It's all over bar the shouting.

'He's just a big ignorant fucking computer fixer,' he explodes. 'What's there to be frightened of?'

She takes her jacket from the back seat and takes his envelope out of the inside pocket. She hands it to him and starts the engine.

'What's this supposed to mean?' he asks, holding the envelope like a distasteful animal.

'You wrote it. You gave it to me. You asked me a question that's your answer.'

'That's cheap.'

'Look, John. You know nothing about me. You think you do but you don't. You have some romantic dream about the two of us setting off on our own, making a new life, settling down to a college tutor's salary. Let me tell you this, Paddy would never let us get away. We'd never escape. He'd eat us for breakfast. Besides I'm tied to him. Tied in more ways than one.'

He stares at her. 'You're ending it aren't you?'

'Yes. I am. I've had enough. I've had enough of your fumbling. Enough of men. I'm sick of all of you.'

'No. You're frightened. You said you were.'

She switches the stereo on. Merle Haggard's aching voice. She turns it off again.

'What does he do to you? He has a hold over you, hasn't he?'

'It's not him.'

'Who?'

'Nobody now,' she says. 'Ghosts. He has a way of finding out ghosts. They all have. That's what gives them power.' *I promised your poor father. He asked me on his deathbed. I'll look after you child.*

'Alice,' he says, 'I can save you. I can take you away.'

'What?' she says. 'Through the power of love?' She laughs aloud. 'This isn't a fairytale.'

And, she is thinking, that is why you fail, John. A

little person who wants to think the best of people. A lover, no more, lost in books and drink and shallow friends. Pain or power are the only things to catch me.

'Oh my dear,' Billy Cleary says. 'Come in. Come in. What happened to you?' His flat is above the Galleria Clary. It is the first time she has stepped inside the door.

It is a comfortless room. A hard three-seater couch in imitation leather, two easy chairs, a fireplace with an electric fire in it. The bright clothes he wore by day, the colourful jacket, the silk bow-tie, hang from a wire that stretches across the far side of the room. The shoulder of a satin dinner jacket she has seen once bulges from the door of a small plywood wardrobe. The television flickers in the corner. A late-night movie. There is a smell of cooking, something processed. Steak and kidney pie. A greasy plate and a teacup on the coffee-table before the television.

'Who did this? Will I get a doctor?' Billy Cleary fusses about her, panicky, fluttering hands and making faces, unable, despite his concern, to touch her. 'I'll phone Hennessy. He comes out at all hours.'

'It's all right Billy,' she says. 'I'm all right now. I just came over because – because I couldn't think of anywhere else.'

'You're bruised.'

'I'm bruised all over Billy.'

'Tell me about it.'

She shakes her head. 'Better not say. But I'm going to get him somehow. I'm not going to let anyone do this to me. I should have known.'

'He's a rough type whoever he is.'

'Oh Billy! You're a complete innocent really. Please. Make us a cup of tea.'

Billy sits on the coffee-table dabbing a handkerchief

at her eyes. She sits there, prim, legs together. I must look a picture, she thinks. Little Miss Moffat sat on a tuffet. She is crying and he is mopping up her tears and in between she blurts out the story in small hard knots, twisting up her body to express them, grimacing.

'I always fall for people like him,' she is saying. 'Why can't I find someone nice like you.'

'You have found me Sandy,' he says. All his camp is gone now. It is as though stepping through his door she passed through the persona, past the mirror that threw back what everyone expected, into his other self. She looks around the room again, wondering where in all this ordinariness was the art dealer, the hustler, the networker to be found?

'No. You know what I mean.'

'I know,' he says kindly. 'You mean you can make love to him and not to me.'

'No. No. That's not it.'

'That's it sure enough. And, in case you get any ideas, it's true. Hands off. I'm strictly mono-sexual. But we're still friends. As it happens, it's a friend you need now. I think.'

'What am I going to do?' she wails. 'Billy what am I going to do?' Now he puts his arms around her, leaning forward to get close enough, his bony shoulders close to her face. 'It's all right child,' he says. 'It's all right.'

'That doctor I went to see, you remember. You gave me his name. He's only around the corner.'

'Hennessy. Yes.'

'He was really telling me that it was all in the mind.'

'What? The pain? Rubbish.'

'No but everything. Why I fell for Paddy. All this – punishment. It was because my father walked out.'

'Listen child,' Billy Cleary says, 'why do you think I only go for men? It *is* all in the mind. Everything. That's what it's all about. Love is a mind game. Only it's a game where you never learn the rules.'

'I just have no faith in myself any more.'

He laughs. 'I believe in one God,' he says, 'the mother almighty.' She smiles. The smile is painful. 'You're an awful bastard,' she says.

Chapter Eleven

'Why are we bringing her?' she asks. They are waiting at the dock for the club ferry to pick them up. In the mirror of her sunglasses his eyes flicker. 'Because we need crew. Billy Cleary told me that she needed a day out.' It is a lie, but not an obvious one. Billy Cleary was evasive when Paddy phoned the gallery. He didn't know where Sandy was. He didn't think she'd be at work for a while. She had had a bad fall. The insinuation was obvious. The little bastard knew. Paddy was possessed of an unwelcome vision: Billy Cleary helping Sandy up the steps of a courthouse. There is a barrister in tow, one of Cleary's crowd – people like him know everyone – an arty-farty barrister who buys pictures of blots, someone for whom Sandy is a cause. Software Tycoon Beats Mistress: Huge Settlement. He had to have her then, somewhere in his sight, somewhere he could assess her mood. Without Cleary she would not do anything he felt sure. But people like Cleary are unpredictable. And they want to punish people like him.

'She's not here.' The little bastard could only lie effectively about art. But he had a chain on the door and short of kicking it in Paddy could not see how he could get past him.

'Look,' he said. 'I'm in trouble Billy. Business trouble and wife trouble. I think I'm going to – well I think Alice and me might be going our own ways. I have to see Sandy. I have to put things straight.' He wondered what Alice's reaction to that would be. Surprise first. He didn't think Alice would go for it. She knew what side her bread was buttered on. But people like Billy were *sympathetic*. That was the defining characteristic of their human relationships. It was the kind of lie he would swallow.

Then Sandy appeared at the top of the stairs. He could see her through the narrow slit the chain left. 'Let him in Billy.'

He drove her back to her flat, searching for some way to bind her to him. 'Come sailing with me tomorrow,' he said desperately. He had uttered the words without thinking about it – the first time he had even thought of risking her in the open. 'Come out for the race. I have the perfect excuse. I'm short-handed. I'll say I bumped into Billy and he suggested you.'

'And what will we say about this?' Sandy said, touching her cheek. Her voice was cold.

'Oh Jesus,' he said. 'I can't believe I did it.'

'I can,' she said. 'I can feel it.'

'I'm under pressure,' he said. 'I'm in trouble. Look, did you hear what I said to Billy Cleary? I'm leaving her. I have to get out. I can't stick her any longer.' The implications were there. He did not spell them out. But Sandy knew she was included.

'Please,' he said. 'Come out on the boat. We'll be together at least.'

The idea had mollified her a little. It was a risk and she knew it. It gave credence to what he said about splitting with Alice. Shortly afterwards she said, 'Is it true?'

He shook his head slowly, the hurt husband, the betrayed. 'There's nothing between Alice and me any more. Not for a long time. She's cold. Icy cold. I won't be sorry to see it over.'

'Billy helped me out. I was in bits.'

'Billy's a good sort,' he said. 'And there's no danger there.'

She swivelled in the seat and looked directly at him. 'That's so crude.'

'I meant he wouldn't do what I did.'

'I know what you meant.'

'He means well.' But he was thinking: interfering little runt.

'You don't know the first thing about him.'

He reached his left hand over and squeezed her thigh. 'I've been worried about you. Jesus, what came over me? I'm an animal. How could I hurt you? It was Nora dying I think. That's the conclusion I came to. We were at college together. We were close at one time. I watched her destroy herself all these years, but I never thought it would come to suicide. I think I was angry at her.' But she was silent. It was not enough. He would have to keep close to her, keep Cleary out, get her to talk. Talk was the key. She would talk herself into believing him. 'I need you Sandy. I love you. Forgive me.'

'Billy Cleary said she loves sailing. That was a lie anyway.' Alice follows his gaze and her glance takes in Sandy's fashionable and useless shoes, her light shirt, her ginger balance on the floating dock. 'You can see she's never been on a boat before,' he says. 'Never trust a queer.' Alice's liberalism is the familiar target but today she is indifferent.

'I'm dropping her after today. I'm not taking her any

more. If I wasn't stuck . . . Where are those dozy bastards?' He scanned the crowd for the two crew that had been able to make it.

Alice shrugs. 'Whatever you want. I don't care.'

Paddy thinks of the day he drove back to the farm, hoping that she would be there. The excitement. He had resisted for years the temptation to go back, to see, to find out. He told himself Sheila was a once-off. But the fantasy plagued him. *There is another one*, it said. *Another chance.* And the day was propitious, the farm even more run-down, the mother as ignorant as ever. And when he saw her the visceral response was overwhelming. She was a beauty, even at that age, a beautiful soiled animal. All his instincts had been proved right. Would you like to come for a spin? To Killarney? A shrug. I don't mind.

Now she is a long way from the small farm – an elegant object, a decorative wife for a wealthy man, self-possessed, assertive, cold. There is none of the dung of the farmyard about her. None of the vulnerability. Paddy looks at her with distaste.

'In a pet now,' he asks. 'Fuck you. Here's the ferry.'

Paddy has been angry for days, a state of perpetual irritation that fused at times into something dangerous. She has seen him like this before – whenever a tricky manoeuvre was needed, a stock market double-deal, a section closure to be negotiated, lay-offs. But usually, within hearing range of the yacht club he switches to business-mode, handshaking and ho-hoing, working potential business partners or clients like a politician. Something else is driving him today.

They troop down the dock and step on to the ferry. Their weight tilts it up and down. The last to board is John, thin, wearing shorts and sneakers, exposing pale grey hairy flesh, out of place. 'He won't be much fucking good,' Paddy says. 'Not much weight there. And he can't sail, can he. I'll have to find something harmless for the bastard.'

'He'll hear you.'

'Who gives a shit!'

'Well it wasn't my idea to bring him. She brought him. So blame her.' And it was true. Paddy could barely contain his fury when Sandy suggested it. She knew some-one, a college friend, who could do with a day out. He was on a postgrad scholarship and never took a day off. If he needed crew, she'd phone him up and ask him. A day out, for Christ's sake. What did she think a yacht race was? He knew what she was doing: safety in numbers, a buffer. The boy was insurance. But he was acutely aware of the need to placate her, to keep her with him, separate her from Cleary. 'Bring him along,' he said cheerily. 'The more the merrier. As long as it makes you happy.'

'Anyway,' Alice adds, 'you said yourself she's completely useless too. Look at her shoes. They'll kill her on a wet deck.'

Alice is irritated that John has found another way to be near her. Sailing is the one uncomplicated thing in her life. On the water she is clear of all her concerns. Even her relationship with Paddy is uncontrived there. It is the one thing they both love, for different reasons.

But now she remembers inviting him herself, the night of the exhibition. Come sailing. You can be near me. They were sitting in the darkness. And now he is here, exactly as she had wished. Except that everything is different. One look, one false move. But, she told herself, Paddy would never know. Paddy didn't see other people. Couldn't read them. John could take his clothes off and fuck her on the foredeck and Paddy wouldn't notice. Not as long as the race was on.

At the last second two trim youths in bright shorts and Heineken T-shirts race down the dock and throw striped bags into the boat. They leap elegantly after them. 'About fucking time,' Paddy says. 'I was going to sail without you.'

'Sorry Skip,' one of the boys says. 'I was taking a leak and I lost track of time.' The other sniggers. They look around them. One winks at Sandy.

The ferry pulls away from the dock, the boatman gunning the engine out of its own tiny smoke-cloud, the smell of diesel and burning oil. The boat slips into the stream and goes up-river. The radio crackles with pre-race chat, the shifting of buoys, lay-lines, crash boats. The water around them is busy with small-craft, people hoisting sails, laying out lines, unmooring. Paddy waves to acquaintances as he passes them at their moorings.

Alice notices that Sandy Muldoon is not wearing a bra, the convex outlines ending in a sharp nipple. When they met on shore they did not feel the need to shake hands and Sandy Muldoon had been unable to meet her eyes. Instead she had looked entreatingly at John. Alice had known then that vulnerability was her weapon. A dangerous one.

One of the boys is talking to John. She guesses he is assessing his experience. She sees him lose interest, his eyes lift to the passing boats. After a few moments he turns his back and waves to a friend. When the friend is past he does not turn back.

Solution is ahead of them, a hull gleaming in the sun. Her lean shape is elegant and aggressive at once. It is a kind of perfection, Alice thinks, to combine both qualities in one object. But closer there is a scum of brown at the waterline and a fuzz of weed. She catches Paddy scowling at it. The weed will make a difference, a fraction of a knot, to the boat speed. But even small fractions count for Paddy.

After the starter-gun the race spreads out and heads for open water. Inside the shelter of the headland breaks the wind, but racing clouds tell her that ahead everything will be faster, riskier, more exhilarating. She can see broken water, a fishing boat with four anglers in it, bobbing and twisting ahead. They will regret chartering on a day like today, but the sunshine fooled them. At sea sunshine is only a surface gloss. Bad weather is all the more dangerous with the bright disguise. They will be heaving their breakfasts out in an hour.

She is familiar with this local see-saw. The race begins in the shelter and the first mile or two is in light airs. Then suddenly, like falling through into a different world, the shelter is removed, the sea builds, the wind screams. Now every move on the boat has to be calculated. Here fingers are lost in winches, booms crack skulls and rope runs screaming through the hands searing the skin away. The downwind leg is a thunderous spinnaker run, then they head back for shelter and begin all over again.

When *Solution* spins round the mark and Paddy calls for the spinnaker, the boat is rearing on the back of a long swell and spume from the wave-tops is blowing away downwind and hitting the sails like shot.

A few minutes together on the foredeck struggling to douse the spinnaker – something safe for John to do according to Paddy – the huge multicoloured balloon sail burbling and filling and exploding out of their grasp. John tells her that he is abandoning his thesis. Giving up college. Getting a job. The news comes out in gasps. The sail thrums and enfolds them, blows away again, gradually dies in their hands until they have it under control and Alice is packing it deftly, systematically into its hoist bag. 'It won't make any difference to me,' she tells him. 'You should stay with your study.'

'I don't care any more,' he says.

'Don't be so bloody dramatic,' she tells him.

Solution is reaching again. She is Paddy's glory. He lavishes the best of everything on her. Today is a bad day, a ham-fisted crew, skipper off form and preoccupied, and still she leaves everything else in her class behind. He stands at the portside wheel watching the telltales on the genoa. North Sails. The latest technology. When he's not watching the sails he's watching Sandy Muldoon, sitting out on the windward deck, her legs hooked over the side. She has taken some spray and her shirt is almost transparent, those sharp breasts standing out when she braces herself. He thinks of *Solution* driving into the swell. It's like rutting, he thinks, not for the first time. The drive and power. Burying yourself. Punishing. Pushing hard. That wimpy student is beyond her, a complete washout who will never learn the ropes. He will question Sandy later, find out why she really brought him. He suspects it is to annoy him. She is punishing him. Two can play that game. Or perhaps it really is protection, safety in numbers. The thought excites him now. Sandy fears him.

Beyond the boy is Alice. Excitement in that too – the risk, the danger. His two women in the same small space. He feels in control, powerful. His mistress and his wife. There are deeper connections also – he knows that. There is something in Sandy that was in Alice, something he hasn't yet reached. Alice was easier. She was a talker, but Sandy has a wound that he can smell but not see.

Sandy watches Alice. More than once she has stood close to her. He's sleeping with me, she wants to say. He's walking out on you. For me.

She turns her face up to the sun and feels its warmth on her bruised cheek.

When she is near Alice she can feel the cold. There is a front of hard air around her. Sandy thinks she can touch it. But the eyes puzzle her. Once when she took her sunglasses off there was a look in them, a small girl look, something frightened.

What did John see in her?

Paddy's right hand is on the wheel, adjusting to the movement of the boat, tiny movements like twitches. It is as though the hand is not part of him, an automaton. The hand that struck her face.

In the lee of the headland again, second time round the course. *Solution*'s chocolate-cream sails are curved to the wind. The perfection of aerodynamics and aesthetics in harmony. The aerofoil filling without a ripple. The boys are watching the sails, sheets in hand, making tiny adjustments on some esoteric principle. The swish of the hull moving through the smoother water. Paddy and Alice are sitting on the high side, feet braced against the inclination of the deck, his hand on the wheel. Her face shines with the joy of the act, bright sunlight reflected off the water.

Paddy is grim.

'The flotation isn't working out,' he says. 'The whole thing is in danger of backfiring.' Not quite true. But he does need to square the circle by moving stock. It is the final move. A matter of a change of name.

Who gives a shit, she is thinking, on a day like this. It'll work out for him anyway. It always does.

'I want to offload stuff.' He takes his eye off the luff for the first time in almost an hour and glances around at the opposition, all swishing steadily towards the mark, slightly astern of them. Then he looks at Alice. 'Into your name. Your maiden name.'

She is alert at once. 'Why?'

'I don't want to explain.'

'You want to put it in my name and you don't want to explain?'

'You never took an interest before.'

She sits back against the guard-wires and stretches her legs. The sun gleams on them. An ancient-looking ketch is drifting on the tide. The colours remind her of Tim Bredin's picture of the hooker. In the end Paddy didn't want it and Bredin had been devastated.

The people on the ketch walk up and down her decks as though out for a Sunday stroll, making no impression on her massive solidity. Sandy and John are chatting low down in the leeward corner of the cockpit, breaking the rule of keeping the weight on the high side. She supposes they are talking about college. Light falling on Sandy's cheekbone delineates a faint cherry – a bruise? John looks frail, almost transparent. Hurt, no doubt. Yet he had come at Sandy's bidding. Alice is touched by his need to be near her, how he is studiously avoiding looking at her, throwing Paddy off the scent, no doubt. He is not to know that Paddy has no concept of other people's lives. John has no function in Paddy's system. She thinks of that night when he was above her, propped on his arms, curved backwards, and his glorious cockcrow: 'We are the lords of summer Alice.' But they *were* deprived of all hope. And they were not gods. It comes to her now that John is ordinary: nothing marks him out but his ability to love and live a decent life. Whereas she is chosen, consecrated. A blessing and an expiation at once. She had been so for Bennis and for Paddy. Once, once in all the years Bennis had told her she was beautiful. When was that? She remembers the phrase now but not the context, a bud burgeoning out of darkness. A weed. *Beautiful. Ah you're a real beauty. What would I do without you.*

The words trouble her now.

She forces herself back to the present and hears Paddy explaining the procedure for the transfer of stock. She cuts him short. 'It's illegal so,' she says. 'You wouldn't need me otherwise.'

She senses the anger rising in him, and the desire to provoke thrills her. To drive him over the edge. 'What are you up to this time?'

'Look,' he hisses. 'I just need a fucking signature, right? You don't know the first thing about it anyway. Any of it.'

Alice looks at him and sees the weird flattened shape of herself thrown back at her from his sunglasses, her own glasses enlarged like insect eyes, gleaming on her face. Then, beyond the barrier of glass she sees that he is old – a heavy-faced man with incipient double chins, a slack mouth, a paunch in the red of his Slam polo-shirt. She is suddenly aware of an image clawing up from memory, a tumour of fear and anger bulging through the skein of consciousness. Sunglasses. Black-framed sunglasses. She sees a hand catch them and take them off, dropping them into something that is soft, almost silent. Cloth? No. Grass? Heather? She hears the tiny creak of the fall. The twist of the hands across the face and sunglasses coming away. But she cannot see the face behind it. The glasses do not reveal a face. No eyes. She feels her stomach twist – the long-forgotten spasm. A nightmare. She forces it back, forcing herself to think of the boat, the sails, the course. Make me cold again, she prays, make me forget. Then she stares at the passing water and tries to see down into its depth and is repulsed.

Paddy is on the foredeck yelling at John. The race has cleared the harbour again and struck steep breaking seas that have another element of venom in them. The tide has turned and now the sluggish undercurrent is slowing the whole mad racing ocean, tripping up the driving waves, tumbling them. Alice sees a wall of water coming at them and collapsing. *Solution*'s bow rises on the square face and breaks through in a confetti of foam. There is a moment of hanging in air, the bow clean out of everything, the wave hissing and growling astern. Then the breath-stopping plunge down the back of the wave, and she buries her bow and green water scoops along the sidedeck ready to suck someone out. Alice stares ahead, riveted by the thought that a false move here would put two men overboard. She could kill Paddy. She sees his black outline against the glaring water, a monster, a leviathan plunging through her days and nights. The rest of the fleet is scattered and labouring in the head-sea. What were her chances? Fifty-fifty or better.

But she would kill John too.

'That ignorant bastard Hennessy,' he says later. 'Guess what he did.' But she has lost interest. She is watching a rival boat trying to set a spinnaker in a desperate attempt to make gains on them, a huge curling balloon, a tangle of garish colours. 'Look at that,' she says. 'A spinnaker this close to the wind. They haven't a clue.' And in the back of her mind is the image of Paddy flashing astern in a welter of white water, one arm upraised like a dorsal fin, a look of surprise on his face.

'You can't trust doctors,' he says. 'They all know each other. It's like a fucking Masonic lodge.' He spits into the air.

Sometimes he would drive fast, abandoning caution, the car twisting and turning on narrow roads. It was a kind of aggression. He liked to throw her around. She would fall against the door or fall inwards on to him and he would laugh and accelerate. She could have ended every-thing then, a quick flick of the wheel. But such an action requires despair or foreknowledge and she was too young for despair. She did not know how deep it all was, how long it would last. She did not know the damage, the loss. If she had been able to tell that her heart would die somewhere along the road she would not have cared about the rest. But the car hurtled on and she lived and it brought her to this point. She saw the oneness of it now, the unity of the journey, the continuum. She had passed from one to another: from a car ticking in the snow of a black night, opened across the top like a tin can, to a car that had an inside only, from which there was no escape, and finally to Paddy's screaming Merc, careering across deserts she could never have imagined. Car to car like a streetwalker until the final stop. Look-ing back from this arid juncture the country road and the winter's night seemed impossibly distant. A small child stood there, staring bleakly at a stranger, wondering how many times she could skip, doing the reckoning. It was Alice, it was Sheila. Two ghosts.

The final hoist that should bring them close on the wind headed for the line. John messes up. The halyard is snag-ged around a spreader and all his cranking and winding and flicking won't free it. Crew on the sheets and guys, shouting. Paddy hands the wheel to Alice and goes forward barking, 'Get off the fucking deck.' With a deft movement of his wrist he brings the rope back in line. The sail goes up, a shadow against the sun, and fills with wind. He hears the cautious grinding of the winch, Sandy trying to be useful. Then the student is standing between the mast and the sail looking useless. 'Get out of the fucking slot,' Paddy yells. 'Get down there and sit down.'

John leans forward and whispers and the breeze carries his words away. He says, 'I fucked Alice.' But Paddy only hears the name. He stares. 'What did you say?' But John shambles down on the leeward side, his feet sliding against the toerail and slips aft on his backside to the safety of the cockpit. What kind of a look is that, between Alice and him? Sympathy? Complicity? The thought occurs to Paddy for the first time in years that Alice has a life of her own, that she is not an extension of him. He wonders what she does with her time when he's not around, and how much she knows or cares about his own activities. Alice, pale and strained at the wheel, steering jerkily, out of synch with the sea and wind, a thing he has never seen in her. If he did not know her better he would think she was seasick.

Her stomach hurts when she moves. Sandy remembers the weightless body of the woodlouse in the dust of the carpet. The sound of Paddy's satisfied breathing. The first blow. She remembers the blood on his shorts. She watches him sullenly.

Cold water on her shirt. The wind has penetrated to the bone and her teeth are chattering. John found a light jacket somewhere and threw it over her shoulders but the shivering is inside.

Something in the cold, the noise, the plunging and cracking of the boat has pushed her into another state. She feels reckless. She thinks of the crazy woman, Nora Delany, driving all the way to that empty farmhouse and then lying down in the rat-hole to die. She could have driven over a cliff. Into a river. Crashed at ninety miles per hour. The huge mass of the BMW, a hammerblow, an explosion of glass and steel. And instant death. Instead she chose to lie down like a child and take her medicine. Somewhere inside of her is a bruise. She nurses it tenderly against the movement of the boat. She feels light. Delicately counterpoised. Ready.

'The one thing you don't do is stand in the fucking slot, right?' The crew snigger, wink at each other and look away.

John shrugs. 'I wasn't aware there was a slot.'

Paddy makes a fist and shakes it at him. 'Don't you smart-ass me!'

Alice says, 'They're gaining on us.'

Paddy whirls. 'We're giving them time and plenty of it. That mess might cost us the race on handicap.'

John shrugs again. 'Sorry.'

Alice is hurt for him. She spits out, 'You're wasting it Paddy, bullshitting!'

'Sorry my arse,' Paddy says.

The wind has shifted, curling around the headland, ruffling the shelter. The run is a short one now, not worth flying the spinnaker. The boom is swung far out, the headsail goose-winged on the other side. Paddy swings up on to the deck to adjust the cunningham, and for an instant he is vulnerable. Alice flicks the wheel. Wind nibbles at the edge of the sail. Suddenly there is a bulge on the outer edge. A crack and the huge aluminium boom is sweeping back across the deck. Two years ago a man was killed this way. An accident.

Paddy's head is at the right level.

He is going to die, she thinks. The boom is going to crush him. In that instant she imagines his sunglasses crashing between the metal and his skull.

Reality stretches. Telescopes. The time between the flick of the wheel and the swing of the boom is one second, maybe two. But she feels she has time to review everything. Thoughts expanding. He is going to die.

But some instinct makes him look. He feels, perhaps,

a loss of urgency in the boat as the wind gets behind the sail. A slight straightening.

He looks and sees death coming at him and he drops to the deck. As he falls he hears the weird cracking and humming of the boom as it sweeps overhead. Jesus Christ! he thinks. Close!

The gybe almost shakes the mast out. The whole boat shudders. Time is normal again. Alice screams, 'Look out!' although he is already safe. A tremendous rattling. And Paddy swearing, dropping back into the cockpit, staring at her. 'Jesus Christ Alice!' he shouts.

I did it, she thinks later. Although it didn't happen. A fracture between the intention and the event. But I did it. I almost got the bastard. Her hands tremble. Her heart exults, thundering in her chest. She thinks of Bennis sneering when she said she would not travel with him again. *You'll be back my lady.* She would have killed him then if there had been a weapon. But there was nothing. He rolled his window up as he drove away. He was leaning forward cranking the handle and she thought of the door of a tomb she had seen in a film about ancient Egypt. The door came down and sealed the tomb for five thousand years. The dead air. The silence. Outside, the crackling desert and the stars.

'You almost fucking killed me!'

A basic mistake. Involuntary gybe. Paddy does not turn his back on her. He swears at the crew, at John especially. 'Get off your arse and tail on that sheet! Pull!' They cross the line. 'That's our worst time this season anyway,' he says. 'Thanks to everyone on board.'

The land is cooling and sucking air from the sea. In the lee of the headland the boats are coming together. The last gun has signalled the last boat. Voices call across the water.

He watches her.

Ice settles on Alice.

She sees them now, two shadows on a hill. The stony hillsides of home. Limestone winks out of every ripple on the hill's blind face. The intricate fretwork of lichen and moss, the gleaming streams. Waterhen and snipe in the valleys, larks in the hungry grass. The fox picking over broken ground. Who are the shadows? One is a priest, the black sweep of the soutane. Can she hear the sound it makes as it brushes the heather? A crow picks over carrion: a little blood, a little exposed flesh. Its wings snap like coarse cloth in a wind. Father Bennis sweeps down on her out of memory, darkening everything.

At first she thinks the other is her father, coming from the high fields where the sheep wandered and fell, where they lambed in isolation and lost young to the cold. Sometimes he brought a pale bundle to be warmed by the fire and fed on warm milk and whiskey. The lamb smell in the kitchen. But something in his gait is different – jaunty, confident: there is no defeat in it. Then she knows that it is Paddy. But Paddy and Bennis were never together. She took care of that. This is a trick of the mind, the unconscious at work. There never was a day when the two of them looked down on her from the same height.

She knows what it means.

From car to car like a streetwalker.

They have the same face now, she thinks. Paddy is getting old. He is getting the jowls and wattles of the contented priest. Good feeding. All the faces in all the cars. All the men on hillsides. What would I do without you? A child skipping. And counting. You'll be back.

'Take the bowline will you,' Paddy calls and she picks up the rope and steps automatically on to the dock. She feels like a machine responding to programming, executing instructions. There are calls of congratulations from the passing racers, obscure challenges, rueful remarks. She hears them as static, noise in the data. When her feet touch down she feels heavier, as though something inside has acquired mass – a colossal tumour, a gigantic child. She feels as though she will drop straight through the timbers. She hits the dock at the same time as Sandy, each of them holding a rope. For a moment their eyes meet and Alice recognises her.

'Cleat the fucking thing!' Paddy shouts as the boat drags along the dock, fenders bulging like pregnant bellies.

They wind the ropes and straighten, still watching each other. Alice says, 'Your shirt is wet.'

'It'll dry.'

'You'll catch cold.'

'It's a warm day.'

Alice shrugs. 'Suit yourself.'

'I saw what you did.'

'You saw nothing.'

The engine dies and Paddy throws some things into the cabin. With studied care he steps off the boat and calls the boatman. He gives him a ten pound note. 'You'll take her up to the mooring yourself Des? The lads'll have her tidied up in ten minutes,' he says, squeezing the note into his palm. 'Have to see a man about a dog.' He makes a drinking gesture with his right hand and the boatman smiles and winks. Then Paddy walks away without looking back, another gesture that has served him well.

Chapter Twelve

They do not drink in the club bar. Paddy says the only reason to drink in the club is to hear the result and he already knows that. But she detects the trace of anger in the thin streak of his mouth, in the narrowed eyes. They go instead to a small place about a mile away. The Hunters Arms. Fake wooden walls. Fake beams. Mock Tudor. What is decent is pastiche. Over-priced drink. A timber sign swings from a wrought-iron bracket. It depicts a bulbous young woman in the arms of a man dressed in what looks like an Edwardian golfing costume. His fowling-piece, leaning against the edge of the sign, makes it clear that the pub is named for his arms. 'What'll you have?' A pint. Two pints. A gin and tonic. A brandy.

They take them to a table that is too small, four sets of knees knocking against each other.

'What brought you out here?' Paddy asks. John smiles weakly.

'I was told you needed a crew.'

'You can't sail, can you?' Paddy says.

The student shakes his head. 'First time ever in a sailboat.'

'It's a fucking yacht actually.'

Coldly. 'First time ever in a fucking yacht.'

Paddy stares, not sure how to respond. 'Enjoy it?' He had tried very hard to get him wet when he was standing on the bow desperately trying to douse the spinnaker. If it hadn't been for Alice he might even have gone overboard. It would have been worth losing the race for that. She had steadied him when the bow sawed sideways and the boat fell down the front of a steep-faced wave.

'I did actually,' the student says.

'What's this your name is again? Paul is it?'

'John.'

'Well John. You had an easy day of it today. A bit of sun makes all the difference. If I had you out on a bad day you'd know you were alive.'

'I do know I am alive.'

'By Jesus, you could have fooled me.' Paddy stares at him. He is still trying to piece together that whisper.

The hostility has gripped everyone. Sandy is staring panic-stricken at John. Alice is wound tight. 'He should have had a lifejacket,' she says. 'Everyone needs to think about flotation. You could sink without trace.' The jibe strikes home. She sees a flicker of anxiety on Paddy's face.

Another round of drink. Paddy's is a double this time. Sandy wonders how much a boat costs. 'Do you have any idea how much that machine out there cost?' Paddy asks. 'I wouldn't like to tell you.'

'Thousands,' Sandy says.

'One hundred and sixty-three thousand pounds sterling,' he says. 'Of course I recovered part of it as advertising. Peanuts. And that was cheap. Second-hand. I don't mind second-hand stuff,' he says, looking at Alice. 'A lot of people only buy new. Me. I like the feeling that other people have been in there. A ghost in the place.

The thing is, it's broken in. Plenty of gear on board that the other fellow put there. Instruments and so on. Then, I knew her race record. Fast. She won in Cowes Week two years ago. The poor bastard had a problem. He had to sell.'

'His daughter fell overboard,' Alice says. 'She was drowned in an offshore race. A perfect opportunity. Paddy likes to make a killing.'

Paddy almost hit her for that. 'Fuck you too,' he says. He tosses the brandy back and goes for another.

'Careful Alice,' Sandy says. 'He's getting steamed up.'

'How would you know?' Alice spits. 'He's my husband.'

Sandy looks away. The place is filling up, locals mixed with yachties. Men in denims smelling of farmyard, and boys in shorts smelling of sunblock. Paddy comes back with a tray. 'Something for everyone. One for everyone in the audience,' he says. It is double brandies all round. 'I forgot the order.' They all know that he doesn't forget.

'Does anybody know anything about the stock market?' Alice asks. The question is deliberate, pointed. She has waited until Paddy is back, seated, lifting his brandy. His glass stops almost at his lips. He waits. Sandy and John shake their heads. Not a thing. No, completely beyond me. Paddy laughs and drinks.

'You're playing a dangerous game,' he says to Alice. 'Watch out.'

'There can't be much to it,' John says. 'It's a form of gambling. All you need is a good start. Money to invest in the first place. You know you probably just need a heap of money. Any moron could play with it.'

'I could do with you in my office sonny,' Paddy says. 'I could give you maybe a quarter of a million to play with. You could make us all rich.'

Sandy laughs nervously. Paddy has lost interest. She sees it in his eyes. Already he is looking around, restless, searching for a target. She has seen it before. One moment he wants to get her clothes off, get her into bed. The next he is shoving a fist in her face, calling her a bitch.

'Where are you from sonny?' he says. John tells him.

'That settles it so,' he says. He is staring at Sandy. 'I have to go into the office. Alice can take you home in her car. Can I drop you someplace Sandy? You're living near the gallery?'

Sandy shakes her head abruptly, suddenly frightened. 'No. Thanks. I'm . . . being collected. Billy is collecting me. Thanks all the same.' Her hand touches her cheek where the faint stain of his fist is still visible in certain lights. How did her hand get there? She feels she has no control of it.

'She doesn't want to go, Paddy,' Alice says. 'Not with you anyway.'

'I only offered her a fucking lift,' he says.

'She won't go with you.'

He looks down at his brandy and says, 'Fair enough so. Anyway I have to go into the office.'

They sip their brandies in silence.

'Tell you what,' he says. 'If I'm ever short of a crew again—'

'You'll call them,' Alice finishes.

'Exactly. Give me your numbers. Here write them here.' He takes a small address book and a biro from his pocket. 'I'll write them myself. Sandy?' He writes Sandy's number down. Alice notices that another number on the same page is identical. It is preceded by a company name. SM Comm. Sandy Muldoon Comm. A childish code. Sandy's face is pale, the bruise standing out beneath the make-up. She is staring at the page.

'You already have that number,' Alice says. 'Look. Up there.'

He flips the pages to J. He writes John. 356796. 'Right,' he says. 'I'd better go. I'm off.' He stands. 'Look,' he says. 'I'll save you the trouble Alice. I'll take whatsisname Paul home.'

John protests. Paddy insists. He winks at Alice and she stares coldly back. John finishes his drink and they go out together.

John comes back to get his coat and Alice walks to the door with him. He senses a steely pain in her that makes him want to touch her, to melt her. But she looks him coldly in the eyes. 'It's all over,' she says. 'Don't come near me again. Everything is finished.'

'You sound desperate,' he says. 'I can help.'

'No you can't John. You never could. You're a nice boy. I would have destroyed you.' He shakes his head. 'It's true,' she says. 'I'm poisoned land. A trap. I don't want to see you again.'

'You're so beautiful,' he says. 'What will I do without you?'

'So long Johnny,' she says. 'In a day or two you'll see – everything will be different.'

'Have another?' Alice says. She feels out of control. She shakes her glass at the barman and indicates two. He nods and winks.

'Thank you,' Sandy says. She has been talking about Billy Cleary, telling Alice how kind he is.

'He's so lonely really,' she says. 'Behind it all. Like a little lost boy. Sometimes I feel like a mother.'

'He probably likes that. They do.' Alice hears herself saying it and cannot believe that those are her words. Sandy stares at her.

'Who?' she says.

'Oh come on,' Alice says. 'I didn't mean that.'

'You meant gay people.' Alice nods her head. 'I like him,' she says. 'Old Billy. I'm very fond of him.'

'Buggery. That's what Billy calls it.' They both laugh. 'He's so funny when he gets going.'

'It's not exactly unique to people of his persuasion,' Alice says. She looks straight at Sandy but her eyes water after a few seconds. Sandy is blushing. 'Don't,' she says. 'Billy is my best friend.'

'I'm sorry. I'm just being bitchy.'

'Two double brandies missus,' the barman says. She drops a ten pound note on the tray. 'And keep the change mister,' she says.

'I saw your name in his book,' Alice says.

'Jesus.' Sandy begins to get up, catching the strings of the bag in which she brought her shoes and coat. Then she changes her mind and sits down again. She breathes an audible sigh. 'This may seem strange but—'

'Drink up.'

'I . . . I don't know how he got it.'

Alice twirls her brandy around in its glass, then holds the glass up so that Sandy's face is behind it. 'He probably got it by asking you.' *I always get it in the end. It might be you, it might be someone else. You're the best of them.* 'Why don't you come home with me,' she says. 'He won't be home for hours. He mightn't come at all.'

'Why?'

'Why not? Because we could have a few more drinks. You could sleep over. No need to worry about drinking and driving. Oh, I forgot you don't drive.'

'Billy is collecting me.'

'Let's be straight now,' Alice says.

Two priests come in and are greeted by a third who has been sitting behind an *Irish Times* three tables away. One takes off his sunglasses in a deliberate movement, folding the arms inwards and putting it in his shirt pocket. The black eyes on the black shirt. They sit down and rub their hands together and one makes a drinking gesture and laughs. The one with the glasses gets up again and goes to the bar. 'Billy isn't collecting you at all,' Alice says. 'I'm not a fool whatever about my husband.'

'I couldn't really—'

They talk about health on the way, the noise of the road roaring up through the low floor of the MG, Alice cornering erratically, blowing her horn. Sandy's unexplained pain. Alice suggests acupuncture and Sandy shrugs and says she couldn't afford it. When they pull into the driveway there is no Mercedes in the garage. 'The bastard isn't home yet,' Alice says. Sandy giggles. The brandy has settled on her head like a soft cap that had the property of making everything outside her head soft too. The house is soft. The garden is soft. A mist makes all the furniture and pictures look vague, intimate and remote at the same time. It does not make her feel uneasy. Instead she feels warm, comforted, safe.

Alice shows her around.

The rooms are furnished in a mixture of antique and ultra-modern that seemed to fit together perfectly – a mahogany escritoire with a stainless steel chair, black carpet tiles under an inlaid cherrywood table, a futon by an oak bookcase. Every wall has its picture – paintings, prints, etchings, sketches, drawings – all the media too. For a moment, as she stands in their bedroom, Alice gone somewhere, her mind tries to wrestle with the value of what hangs on the walls alone and the figures elude her. A hundred thousand perhaps. Perhaps less. Certainly a lot of money. She is admiring a small bleak le Brocquy above a Georgian chest of drawers when Alice comes back carrying two glasses. She stands beside her for a moment then hands her one.

'You love art don't you?' Sandy nods.

'I'd love to own just one of these. Just one.'

'Take it,' Alice says. 'That one? Le Brocquy. Would you like that? Or this. That's Hockney.'

'No. You're joking.'

'Please,' Alice says.

Alice sits on the bed and she sits on an easy chair, her back to the window. They sip their drink. Sandy can't quite place the taste – sweet, a long drink with ice in it, and a lemon. Nothing she has tasted before.

'You fuck my husband,' Alice says quietly. Sandy's drink tips into her lap, the embarrassment helping to cover her shock. Alice is up in an instant, fussing, trying to prevent the reddish liquid soaking into the carpet, kneeling in front of her. She stops after a moment and looks up. She straightens and put her arms on Sandy's knees. Her face is looking almost vertically up. Sandy thinks: how beautiful she looks.

'Please don't tell me any lies, Sandy. I know what's happening. And I see he left his mark.' She reaches up suddenly and her fingers brush Sandy's cheek. 'I don't care. In fact I pity you in a way. You can have what I had and welcome. Years of it. Easily enough for two lifetimes. So don't feel you're taking anything from me.'

Sandy shakes her head and bites her lip. She feels close to tears.

'Please. Say it.'

'Yes. It's true.'

'More than once?'

'Yes.'

'How often?' *Father Bennis's lazy voice, unshockable, covering his excitement. How often my child? And then the penance and the absolvo te. And sometimes there were sweets.*

'I don't know. Five or six times.'

'Does he hurt?'

Sandy swallows hard. Alice's hand still rests lightly

on her cheekbone. 'Yes. Yes.'

'He used to beat me.'

Sandy's eyes open wide.

'Yes. Never on the face. He'd never hurt your face if you were his wife. It wouldn't look good. But you're a secret. Even I never guessed. I thought it was all over since he got to be so busy. I thought he had no time for other women.'

'Yes.'

'What did he do? What kind of things did you do with him?' *Tell me everything my child.*

Sandy looks trapped, her eyes searching right and left. She lifts her glass and drinks rapidly. Then she murmurs something. But Alice seems to have lost interest.

'I chose him you know,' she says. 'I decided to marry him. To escape.'

'Did you? Escape?'

Alice shakes her head. 'They're all the same, I think.'

'No!' Sandy says. 'No. I refuse to believe it.'

'I don't mean men. I mean users. They all have the same system.'

'What do you mean?'

'They find the weak ones. They have a nose for it.'

'No. Not me.'

Alice smiles at Sandy. Then she straightens off her knees and kisses her lightly on the cheek, the shadow of the bruise like the suggestion of disease on a leaf.

'People fall into two categories, Sandy. The users and the victims. The users all have the same system. All you have to do is learn it and you're in. You change from being a victim to being a user. Using is what gives you power. All powerful people can turn it on like a tap, and they can be anywhere. It could be a businessman in a suit like Paddy, or a priest, or a general or a politician. The secret is in the nose. They can smell us. The other secret is their contempt.'

She gets up and goes back to the bed.

'The great skill is to know the exact moment of power. Watch Paddy next time. He examines people. He pushes a little, maybe insulting them, maybe pushing some business line with them, probing, testing. At some point he loses interest. You can see it in his eyes. He'll look away. Or he'll order another drink. That's when he knows. Then, unless he wants to screw the person, he switches off. He files them away.'

'Oh Jesus,' Sandy moans. 'Stop. Please.'

Alice lies back and closes her eyes. There is the hint of a smile in the corners of her lips. 'At least we know where we stand,' she says.

A steel-grey sky has lowered on them and the city lights spread like a blush across it. The air is thick. Sandy stands at the window and says it is beautiful. Alice shrugs and cradles a glass to her shoulder. She says: 'Sometimes I think a cloud like that might crack and fall down. Bits and pieces lying everywhere. Like grey snow or giant dandruff. It would crush people. Change things.'

She thinks of dandruff on a black shoulder.

Now they have a bottle of wine jammed between their hips. They are both on the bed. Alice is crying. Sandy is trying to comfort her without spilling the bottle.

'The bastard,' she is saying, over and over. 'The bastard.'

Alice talking about cars, about mountain streams, about horses standing in dark gateways. The bric-à-brac of memory. Suddenly she sees it: He was happy. He had a happy life. All the small things add up. Father Bennis passed his days in contentment among his flock. A decent man. A respected man. And his pleasures were few. And moderate. The golden mean. But it destroyed her.

Now she sees it differently. There were little excursions: to the St Patrick's Day parade, to a play in the nearby town, to the mountains, the seaside. There were treats of ice cream, gobstoppers. He took her out of the rain, through the swashing night, in the heat of his car, and left her at the door safe and sound. Each small thing was perfect in its way. So carefully planned. And each time there was a little pleasure. A small thing. A little reward.

A man of modest demands.

A happy life. A contented life.

'Did you?' Sandy is asking. 'Did you try to kill him that time? On the boat. I saw you turn the wheel.'

'Yes,' Alice says. 'Yes, yes.'

Sandy holds Alice as she spews into the toilet – bile and wine – a haemorrhage through mouth and nose – tears too – she voids herself.

Paddy comes home after midnight. They are asleep by then, the empty bottle lying on its side on the floor. Sandy is on her side faced towards the window and Alice is curled around her, her right arm thrown around her waist.

Paddy steps quietly up to the bed and looks down on them. 'Fucking babes in the wood,' he says. He grips Sandy's hair and pulls her out of the bed. She screams and Alice wakes up and sits upright rubbing her eyes. 'Get out bitch!' Paddy shouts. 'Out of my fucking house!' He still has her hair in his fist. Now he yanks hard and stands her upright. She screams again and puts her hands to her head, trying first to pull his grip away, then to scratch his hands with her nails. He ignores her clawing and drags her to the door of the bedroom. Then Alice is on him from behind, pummelling with both fists. He launches Sandy outwards against the far wall and turns on his wife. He pushes her back to arms' length and strikes her full in the face with his closed fist. She stumbles backwards and her knees give out. She sits down suddenly, blood running from a split lip. He steps outside and closes the door behind him.

Sandy is tumbling down the stairs, crying and holding her head with her left hand. He follows and pushes her the last few steps so that she rushes forward and sprawls on the carpet of the hall.

Alice returns from darkness, the feeling that for a moment or an hour or a year she has been elsewhere. The doorway in front of her looks hazy, soft at the edges. She hears something crying. Someone crying beyond her bedroom door. She thinks she is at home again listening to her father's blind wailing the night of the accident. Then the haze clears further and she becomes aware of the pain in her lip and cheek. Paddy struck her. A full blow. She remembers the feeling of letting go, the fall backwards into silence. Where is he now? She gets to her feet unsteadily and opens the door. There is no one in the corridor but the cries are louder. She can hear muttering too, a kind of shouted mutter but the words are indistinct. She has the feeling that a cellphone is ringing somewhere. She edges along the wall to the head of the stairs and looks down.

Paddy is lying on top of someone in the hallway. His trousers are down to his knees and he is fucking her hard.

Alice thinks it must be Sandy Muldoon. He is a bastard to bring his woman home. Now she can hear what he is saying. 'Fucking bitch! Slut! Fucking slag!' The words are repeated over and over again, hypnotic, a steady drumbeat, timed to his thrusting. And she is saying, 'Please! No! Oh Please.' The glass ornaments on the hall-table are a tiny carillon. A hat-stand is shaking. Alice shakes her head and tries to focus on what is happening but shaking her head only makes her dizzy. She sits down on the top step of the stairs. Then it stops. Paddy sits back on his haunches and slaps the woman across the face. She stops wailing. Then he gets up and pulls his trousers up, and Sandy looks at the top of the stairs and sees Alice.

Alice can see that he has pulled away her shirt so that her breasts are exposed. There is a single shining button on the hall floor like a dreamy eye. There is blood on one nipple. Her shorts are gone too, lying in a bundle by the hat-stand. A crumple of silken rag slightly further away.

She rolls over on to her side and curls her legs up and he turns away. He glances up at Alice and says something that she doesn't hear. Then he comes up two steps of the stairs and says it again.

'Sorted your lesbian friend,' he says. 'I'm going to make a sandwich.'

Alice comes downstairs when he is gone and helps Sandy to her feet. She leads her upstairs and puts her to bed in the guest bedroom. Before she leaves she shows her how to lock the door. Then she locks herself in the spare room.

Chapter Thirteen

Morning. Cold and grey. Wind lifts the skirts of the trees in the garden showing pale underclothing, thread-veins; the startling skin of another kind of life raised unexpectedly to attention. Rain is threatened, low clouds a uniform grey. Sandy sits immobile as Alice applies the Dettol. There are cuts everywhere. Some are bites, some are bruises that have broken. Her buttocks are raw where his thrusting dragged her on the hall carpet. Her left nipple is a huge swollen bite. One side of her head is numb. The worst pain, she says, is inside. She feels split, torn in her vitals, eviscerated.

'How did this happen to me?' Sandy says. 'To me?'

During the night he looked for Alice, drunk himself at that stage. Perhaps four in the morning. He hammered at the door, pleaded, wheedled, begged. Then he tried kicking it. Alice dragged a tallboy against it and the heavy hardwood door held against his inept attack. She shouted at him that he had raped a woman in his own house and he said she was asking for it, that she liked it, that she was a whore. But he didn't go back to Sandy's room. She heard him showering at seven and shortly afterwards, watching from behind the curtains she saw the Merc pull out and drive away. She stood at the window watching the empty drive and saw a thrush breaking a snail on the tarmac. Clack. Clack. The tiny frantic breast. She heard the sound of Sandy's door opening and closing, then opening again. She dragged the tallboy away and looked out. Sandy was standing at the top of the stairs, half dressed, petrified. She did not look round when Alice's door opened.

She closes the Dettol and places it carefully in its place in the First Aid box. They had joked about that box years before – Alice insisting that they have it 'just in case', Paddy saying that a packet of Band Aid would be enough. She had used it often enough since then. 'Get dressed now. Look, I brought these for you.' They are her own clothes. She is bigger than Sandy, but they would fit reasonably well.

'Oh God,' Sandy says. 'I'm going to die.'

'Not of these cuts, not unless you die of shame.' Alice is thinking of a time she had broken a toenail on a stone and Sheila had taken it in her two hands and kissed it.

'The bastard.'

'He is a bastard.'

'Why do you stay married to him?'

'I'm not. I'm going.'

'Oh Jesus Christ, he raped me.'

Alice makes coffee and butters slices of bread and they sit together at the table drinking, ignoring the bread. The rain comes down finally and they hear it hissing on the road and pattering in the leaves and the gutters. A sullen light steals colour from everything.

They hear the sound of distant cars hissing through it.

'I feel like some kind of a dump,' Sandy says. 'Some kind of a bin that people stuff things into. All kinds of shit. An ancient beat-up fucking piss-pot. Like he's been pissing into me for months. How can people do that? All his badness going into me. He poisoned me.'

Alice shrugs and says nothing. The silence of impossible relationships deepening between them.

'He told me he was going to leave you. Divorce.'

Alice laughs. 'He must have been desperate.'

'It was a lie?'

Alice makes a gesture of pinching money between finger and thumb. 'The settlement would hurt.'

Time brings the sounds of people going to work and school. Children calling to each other across roadways, fences, garden sheds, splashing through puddles, and cars, buses, vans – remote intimations of the given world. 'We have to get him,' Alice says at last. How much time has passed. Alice thinks half an hour. It is almost nine o'clock.

'How?' His power is the unspoken obstacle: strength accrued to him by virtue of their pain. She means: How can we possibly harm him? We are the victims.

Alice laughs again. 'Easy. We'll just blow his head off.' The thought seems to cheer Sandy. She laughs first, then tears come again. 'Fuck him,' she says. 'Fuck the rotten bastard.'

'You could go to the guards.'

Sandy shakes her head. 'No. No.'

'You're right. It still makes you the loser.'

Sandy puts her head down on her knees and folds her hands across the top of her head. She rocks herself by lifting her heels off the ground and tilting her body backwards and forwards. It is an animal movement, a foetal response, to fold up and take shelter, to harbour anger and pain, husband energy. A wounded animal can cure itself at times, the secret of healing preserved in some kind of genetic code, but the human has lost the touch.

Alice looks down at her head. 'I'm serious.'

'What?'

'Let's shoot him.' Sandy straightens up again and stares at Alice. 'Don't be stupid.'

Alice goes to the sink. She pours a glass of water, drinks it and comes back to the table. She does not sit down.

'You should do it because he raped you. If you don't I will.'

'What? No! Jesus.'

Father Bennis on the altar, his hand raised in blessing over the congregation. Go in peace to love and serve the Lord. His power was the altar, the gold-encrusted vestments, the polished black shoes and stiff clerical cloth of his coat. My dear brethren.

'I can and I will. There are guns. One of his own.'

Sandy shakes her head and then touches the side where he held her hair. 'You'll go to prison. The two of us. We'll both go to prison.'

'Not if we stick together.'

'You're mad.'

'No. I've thought about it before.' She walks round the table once. She stops behind Sandy and puts her hands on her shoulders. She leans down and puts their heads together. She folds her arms tenderly around her shoulders. 'Listen child,' she whispers. *Just the two of us. We don't need anyone else.* 'We can do it together. The two of us.' Sandy shivers.

'Cold?' She begins to caress her shoulders. 'Stand up.' Sandy stands obediently and Alice turns her round so that they are face to face. She puts her arms around her and holds her tight. Then she kisses her gently, wary of the wound in her own lip.

She leads her out of the kitchen and down the hall. 'This is his office,' she says. She opens the door and they walk in. There are two computers at opposite ends of the room, a large desk with filing drawers beneath, another filing cabinet. The computers whirr, their screens alive with expanding and disappearing webs of lines against a black background. The room holds no pictures, no photographs, no decoration of any kind except over the desk, on hooks on the wall, three shotguns. One is an over-and-under and the other two are side-by-sides. Their handles gleam with varnish. The dull grey of the barrels suit the morning light.

'Guess,' Alice says. 'Which is the best one.' The highest one, a side-by-side has ornate decorations on the stock, swirls and flowers. The stock is well polished. But Sandy points to the lowest one tentatively – a more restrained weapon, oak stock, a subtle rose engraving – not taking her eyes off Alice for long. 'The bottom one?' she says.

'That one is a Purdey,' Alice says. 'Do you know what a Purdey is?' Sandy tries to slip out of her embrace. She looks at the door not the gun. 'I want to go home,' she says.

'A Purdey is a very expensive gun.' Alice remembers how he had found the advertisement through the Internet: J. Purdey classic game gun with typical rose and scroll engraving. Cased in oak & leather case. Price £7,400. He had quoted it so often to her that she remembered it in detail. 'It's his pride and joy. Did you ever smell the barrel of a gun that's just been fired? It's like sex. Acrid. The smell of cunt and semen all mixed up. And sweat.' *It's all perfectly natural between married couples.*

Sandy begins to moan.

'Stop,' Alice says. 'It's over. He's never going to lay a finger on you again.' She puts her free hand on Sandy's belly and pressed gently. 'Never.'

A watery electronic warble silences them. They stare at each other. Then Sandy's face slackens. 'It's Billy's mobile.'

'Jesus Christ! Where's Billy?'

'No. No. It's all right. He gave it to me in case I needed him. He said he'd check up on me. It's in my coat.' They listen until the sound stops. 'He's nice,' Sandy says suddenly, shuddering as she says it, almost in tears again. 'I wish he was straight.'

Alice laughs bitterly. 'He'd be the only straight man in Ireland if he was.'

She pushes Sandy into the office chair. 'That's his seat. That's where he sits when he's working. He does it all by computer. E-mailing. Buying and selling stock. Faxes.' The multicoloured webs grow and shrink, pulsing across the screen, following their own laws. 'It's left plugged in all the time. He never turns it off. It's his way of being in control. Your ass is where his ass sits. You're in his place. Feel the power?' *Put your hand on the gearstick child. The Cortina has great power.*

She reaches over the desk and takes down the Purdey. 'Cover your face,' she says. She points the barrels directly at the screen and swings hard. The glass shatters and sparks. Sandy opens her eyes suddenly and sees that the screen and its webs are gone. The humming is still there. 'Shit!' Alice shouts. 'Shit! Shit! Shit!' She brushes the screen off its pedestal. She tries to shove the barrel of the gun into the disk drive. 'Shit!'

'Just unplug it!' Sandy shouts. Alice shakes her head. She rushes out and comes back a moment later with the coffee pot. She drags the large unit out from under the table and tilts it slightly. Then she pours the coffee into the vents on its upper surface. They hear a fizzling sound and the humming stops. They also hear the fridge going down in the kitchen. 'I fused the lights,' Alice says. They both laugh. 'I fused the fucking lights.'

They get a hammer and smash coin-shaped breaks into the plastic of the two hard drives, the hammer bouncing back with each blow. The glass of a second screen collapses easily, revealing tubes and wires. They smash those. Then they smash the fax and telephone. Their faces glow through the bruising. Alice surveys the damage, the litter of glass and tubing, wires, plastic, circuit boards. 'It's glorious,' she says.

'We did something.'

'It's not enough,' Alice says.

Sandy buckles suddenly. Tears streaming down her face, hands flailing, words streaming spit, she reels across the room and comes to a stop against the wall. Alice drags her back and folds her into her arms, stroking her head, whispering to her. Easy child. It's all right. He won't touch you any more. Never again.

'I'm frightened. I'm frightened,' Sandy says. Over and over. 'I'm frightened.' *I'm frightened Father. No need. It's not a sin if a priest does it.*

'You were frightened last night.'

Sandy moans. 'I fell for him because he looked like my father. I know that.'

'Is that what you think?'

'It's true. My father ran away when I was a kid. I'm always looking for someone to replace him. I've been diagnosed. I'm supposed to go for counselling. Me.'

'I thought I picked him too. I thought I had my reasons.'

'You wanted to escape.'

'That was what I thought. I could tell you things, Sandy. If I chose.'

'I used to be happy. Once I was happy.'

'I told you,' she says, 'we give off our own special smell like bitches in heat. We attract the bastards that're going to use us. They come from miles around.' *I know your type.*

'We'll say it was an intruder. We'll say they raped you and tried to rape me. We'll say Paddy came home and disturbed them and they shot him and ran away.' *I'll say you're making it up. It'll be your word against mine. The word of a priest against the word of a common slut with a record as long as your arm in school. Do you know only for me the good sisters would have sent you packing years ago? What would your mother say?*

Sandy shakes her head. 'They'll take samples. They'll know what time it happened.'

'And they'll match his DNA.' *Father Bennis bought ice cream for me and it melted.*

'They will.'

'We'll pretend we came in and found him. We'll go out now and stay in your flat. We'll come back after dark and sneak in.'

Sandy brightens at the idea. 'And if we're caught I can always say he raped me. I'll say I was insane. That's what they're all saying anyway. The doctor says I should go for counselling.' Alice kisses her on the forehead. 'We'll load the gun and put it back. He won't notice.'

Alice rummages in the filing cabinet and brings out a box labelled Ely Grand Prix 12. She takes two cartridges out and breaks the Purdey. She puts one cartridge in and hands the other to Sandy. Sandy takes it and studies it for a moment. Then her hand starts to tremble and she sticks it in the barrel. For a moment it looks as though it wouldn't go in, then it slides down into the cylinder and Alice closes the gun.

The electronic tinkling starts again. Alice looks at Sandy. 'Where is it?'

'In my coat. Or else my bag. In the kitchen I think. I can't remember.'

'Fuck.' They let it ring. When it stops the front door opens and closes and they hear Paddy's heavy steps in the hall, then in the kitchen. They stop breathing. They hear him calling for her. Then Sandy. He goes up the stairs. They can hear him calling them and saying he is sorry. They hear the door of the guest bedroom open. He'll be studying the bloodstains in the bed, they think. Then they hear him try the spare room. Then the burbling sound of someone pissing overhead. Finally they hear him go into the main bedroom. They hear the bedsprings creak for a moment and then there is silence. *Aah*.

'Oh God,' Sandy says.

'No more fairytales,' Alice says. 'We're going to kill him.' *It's a kind of sacrament with a priest.*

Sandy shakes her head. 'I can't do it.'

'You have to believe in life,' Alice says, quietly. 'To kill someone. You have to believe in the sanctity of life. You have to have faith. Otherwise, it's not worth doing. There's your own life. You have to save that. And then, there's what he did. The punishment has to be enough. It has to stand for all the things that were done to you all your life. All.'

Sandy shakes her head again. She is standing bolt upright, rigid, trembling like a pole in a high gale. 'No. No,' she cries. 'No no I can't.'

Yes yes you little minx. You'll do what you're told. 'We must. If you don't do it I will. I'll do it for you. I'll point it straight at his prick and I'll blow the whole thing off. Remember Bennis raped you.'

'Bennis? You said Bennis?'

'I meant Paddy.'

'No. It's too much,' Sandy says.

'Take it.' She thrusts the gun into Sandy's hands and turns her towards the door. 'Go.' Alice seems paper-thin, transparently white. Her hands tremble, her steps are short, strained, her dark eyes are lit from the inside and glow like fire behind paper.

They move silently along the hallway, walking on

tiptoes like cartoon characters, everything happening in slow-time, and stand for a moment staring up the stairs. They speak in whispers. 'Let the safety catch off,' Alice says. 'There,' showing her. Sandy slips her thumb on to the catch and eases it forward. Alice puts her hands on Sandy's hips and moves her forwards to the step. 'Up. Go.' She can feel Sandy's trembling. She remembers another time, years before. Sheila came in late at night and got into bed. In those days the girls slept in one bed, the boys in another. Sheila was trembling. Her whole body was moving in tiny vibrations. Her breathing was shallow. She remembers her sister's heat in the bed. *Remember your sister Sheila.*

They move slowly up, one stair at a time. At the top Alice whispers, 'Remember the way he slapped you when he was finished. He always likes to hurt you when he's finished himself. He used to do that to me too. A knee between the legs by accident. Or a pinch. He used to bite my neck so that I had to wear polo necks.' Her lips are in Sandy's ear, whispering.

'Me too,' Sandy says. The shaking is less seismic now, her body steadying a little.

'In.'

They go to the door. He has left it open. He is lying on the bed in his shirt and trousers. His shoes are on the floor. His jacket is on the end of the bed. He is asleep, his arms stretched out on either side, his head thrown back, his mouth open. He reminds Alice of the figure on the cross in Father Bennis's car, except that there are no purple spots on his palms and feet. She remembers Father Bennis closing his fist over the figure to blind him. They can hear his breathing, adenoidal, almost a snore. Only in sleep is he open, Alice thinks. No defences. Awake he is secretive, retentive, vigilant. She steps forward and stands in front of him. She hears Sandy's dead footsteps behind her.

Suddenly his eyes open. 'Alice,' he says. 'I came back to say—'

'You fucking bastard,' Alice says. *God's infinite mercy.*

He is sitting up, about to swing his legs out, when the shotgun goes off. Ten feet. Alice sees blood flower suddenly in his right thigh and that leg jerked sideways and outwards, twisting at a crazy angle. Then she sees that the blood was really a redblack gel, a black tennis-ball of macerated cloth and wad and blood and shot. She sees that there is a bulge of flesh above the wound where the force of the shot has pushed a flap of cloth and flesh backwards. Small picks of shot have spattered wider. There is a smoky acrid smell.

'Oh Jesus,' he says. He falls backwards, his head missing the pillow. There is terror in his eyes. 'Oh Jesus Jesus Jesus.'

'Sandy—' Alice begins, but Sandy steps forward. She is looking down at Paddy.

He is staring at her. He is frightened now.

Sandy's lips are curled back off her teeth. She makes a sound like a cat spitting. Alice thinks at first that it is a word. Then that she has actually spat. She smiles and Sandy smiles back, that crude smile, baring her teeth again. 'You destroyed the bed,' Alice says. 'I hate mess.'

'Help me Alice,' Paddy calls. 'She's mad.' Spittle is white at the corner of his mouth. He seems to be salivating. His eyes are wide, pupils dilated.

'You raped her,' Alice says. For an instant she thinks of the untidiness of it all, the blood, the disarray of the bed, the mess of the wound. The old instinct surfacing. Tidy yourself up.

'Not rape,' Paddy wails. His hands are grasping at the fabric of his trousers. She sees his fingers meet the hole, close on the torn edge. He pulls upwards convulsively and she sees the fabric rip. It makes a low-pitched sound, like rain spilling into a gutter. His body is writing, convulsed by pain and shock. Blood grows across the sheet like an inkblot painting, all kinds of unaccountable shapes. A single massive blotch darker near the centre and several unexplained independent spots like drips from the ceiling. 'Not rape,' he says. 'She likes it. Always that way. Jesus Jesus I'm going to bleed to death Jesus.'

'No you're not,' Sandy says. She raises the gun and pulls the trigger at the same time. The shot was intended for his face but she fired while the gun was still swinging up. She would have shot him in the belly but the recoil plucked the barrel upwards and sideways. The shot punches a small hole just to the right of his heart. He buckles, almost rolling on to the wound, and stops moving completely for a moment so that they think he is already dead. Then his right hand moves, a temperate, tractable movement, coming away from the wound slowly, the fingers opening a little, like a man showing a magic trick to a child.

Billy's cellphone begins to ring.

Mick Delany has finally buried the cat. He chooses a place directly under the cherry tree and spends twenty minutes trying to find enough soil between the roots to accommodate a grave. He is reduced, in the end, to scrabbling on his hands and knees, sawing through the roots with a breadknife. Their white flesh reminds him of Nora. He digs out a cat-shaped hole and places the rigid Tilly in it. Unaccountably, he is crying when he fills the earth in. He finds a broken concrete block near the compost heap and places that on top of the mound. Then he walks back to the house and picks up the huge whiskey he had poured earlier. The television rumbles about ethnic cleansing, the flickering blue light. He raises the glass towards the concrete block and says,

'Fuck you too Tilly.' He stands swaying on the edge of the patio, looking up at the lowering evening sky.

He hears the doorbell ringing later when he goes to refill the glass. By then his mind is foggy and he thinks it might be Nora home late from some jaunt or other. When he throws the door open, ready to be angry all over again, it is Alice Lynch. The red MG is half-parked, its tail angled out on to the avenue, the passenger side bumper jammed against the gate pillar. He can see another dent in the door further back.

'Jesus Mick, I'm ringing for ten minutes,' she says. She is excited, he can see that. 'Come in Alice,' he says.

'You're drinking,' she says.

'Not much.'

'I suppose I can understand.'

'That's what you think.'

He leads her into the living room and points at the garden. 'I buried the cat,' he says. 'Where that block is.'

'What are you talking about?'

'She drugged it,' he says. 'Poisoned.' Nora killed the cat, he was certain of that. The cat was part of some kind of terrifying version of life that Nora was experimenting with. The cat was the control. If the cat died, Nora died too. If the drugs she was taking were not sufficient to sustain the cat, her own life was unsustainable. The death of the cat was the signal. He should have been able to read it. But in the end Nora would have found some way, another way, to do it. At least she had the decency not to crash the BMW.

'Mick, listen, I'm in trouble. Listen to me.'

'All have our troubles.'

Who said that before? He can't remember. The light is fading in the garden. A huge gathering of crows is moving slowly across his line of vision. He can hear their racket. A black cloud in the sky, a storm coming towards him or away from him. Hitchcock. A stain in the evening sky. Thundering. The crow symbolises death, he thinks. What's that he read about Hitchcock and that actress – that he caged her up with the birds until they pecked her raw? Good for Hitchcock – get the bitches.

'Paddy is dead.'

He stares at her. 'What? Nora is dead.'

'So is Paddy. That girl shot him.'

He gropes for the remote and flicks the television: Serbia collapsing to a pin-prick of humming light, a black star. He sits down and gazes bleakly up at her. For a minute they stare at each other. Then he looks down at his drink and swills it about in its glass. The silence lengthens.

'Well?' she says.

'Who shot who?' He waves the hand that holds the glass, a circular movement, his index finger extended like a pointer, as if he were pointing at a range of possible suspects.

'The girl. Sandy Muldoon. She shot Paddy.'

'Sandy Muldoon from the gallery?'

'Jesus Christ Mick.'

He makes an effort to concentrate. 'She shot Paddy. Why?'

'Because he raped her. They were sleeping together.'

'Raped her?'

'Look. I came into the house. I heard crying from upstairs. I went up to the bedroom. She was standing beside the bed and he had – he had a hole in his chest. And in his leg I think.'

'Jesus. A hole in his chest. What did you do?'

'I ran. I've been driving around all day. I didn't know what to do.'

'Driving around? Where?' She waves her hand at the outside world, the homing crows, the sullen air, the trees, the neighbours' fences, chimneys, television aerials, the sound of passing cars. 'I don't know. I'm nearly out of petrol.'

'Why didn't you go to the guards?'

He is surprised by her laugh. She says, 'Don't be a fool Mick. You knew the way Paddy and me were. The dogs in the street knew about it I suppose. I hated him. If I went to the guards that's the first thing they'd find out. I'd be suspect number one.' She mimics the solemn voice of a guard giving evidence. 'The deceased was known to beat his wife.'

A shrewd look comes over his face. He is sobering up now. 'You'll have to. Sooner or later. Have to tell the guards. They'll find out anyway.'

She sits down now, stretching her legs on the carpet. She takes her time answering. 'I notice you're not too shocked yourself.'

He drinks most of what is in the glass and swallows it noisily before answering. 'Look Alice, I might as well tell you. Nobody liked him. In fact a lot of people hated his guts. He was only pleasant when he was patronising you. When he was being patronising he was screwing somebody. He fucked me around once or twice I can tell you. I couldn't say he was my best friend.'

Surprise registers as a paler shade in her pale face, a whitening of the eyes. 'You hated him. I thought you were friends since college.'

He looks closely at her and finds that his eyes will not focus properly. Sometimes, he thinks, the women are the last to know. They think their suffering is exclusive, that their hatred is personal. They are the same in love. They think sometimes that they are the first in the history of the world to experience it, hurt if their illusion is exposed. Men have a broader view. They see that lovers come and go and when one goes another can be procured. 'I did. I hated him. I can't say I'm sorry to see the back of the bastard.'

'Why?'

'Too many things to mention.'

'Tell me one. Please.' She tips forward off the chair and kneels in front of him. She rests her hand lightly on his arm. It is a sexual gesture, indicative of something, one that she learned years before. She sees him staring at her fingers. She hears a clock ticking, a light, metallic tick. She hears children shouting nearby. Playing football in the gloom.

'Nora for a start. You probably knew they slept together years ago.' She nods. Paddy often boasted about it. 'Well he kept at her. Off and on. When she was working he used to phone her. When she gave up he started to call here. When her nerves – got out of hand. I often wonder if he was to blame for it. But I suppose he wasn't. The truth is he was always careful.'

'Bastard!'

'I'm sorry Alice.' She waves her hand, telling him to go on. 'I know they were together at least once since. I found a letter he wrote to her. On headed notepaper. One slip in all the years. Even then he didn't sign it.'

'Have you still got it?' He shakes his head.

'Then he got me to buy some stock he was floating at some point. I became,' he phrases the term carefully, 'the subject of discreet inquiries by the stock exchange. Fuck him. I still haven't worked out how he was using me.'

'Join the club.'

He raises an eyebrow at her. 'How much do you want to know?'

'I don't care any more,' she says. 'He's dead.'

'You're very cool, for someone who just saw her husband's mistress shoot him to death.'

'You're talking to suspect number one. And you're not exactly worried. Complicity?'

'You're a beautiful woman, Alice.'

'I know. You should see me in the bath.'

They laugh. 'I'll get you a drink. We might as well be civilised.' He pours a brandy for each of them, topping the glasses up with ginger ale. He hands one to her and she sees that his hand is shaking slightly. 'I'd like it,' he says. 'To see you in the bath.' They laugh again.

'Here's to the bastard,' he says. They touch glasses lightly.

'Did he ever talk to you? About me?'

'No.'

'He didn't tell you anything about me?'

'No. We weren't on speaking terms. Not really. On a business footing maybe.'

'She was badly beaten. You could see that.'

'You said he raped her?'

'That's what she said. Who would have thought it. That she'd kill him for it, I mean.'

'Here's to Sandy.' They drink again. Her eyes fill up with tears. 'I was abused. As a child.' He shifts in his seat, crosses his legs, suddenly uncomfortable. 'By a priest.'

'Jesus.'

'He knew that. I don't know how he found out. Maybe I told him some night when I was drunk. I drank a lot when I was younger. I might have let it slip. Anyway he teased all the details out of me. I hated it. He said it was therapeutic. It would help me to put it all behind me. Fuck him. He's dead anyway. That's the end of it.'

She knew well why he did it. It was his power. Information is power, he often said. He said that was why the computer world was the most important place to be. In the end, he said, we will create the power, have the means to use it, the drive to control. So she knew that his questions meant the same thing. What did he do? How did he say it? What kind of a night? What kind of clothes? Where? Tell me again. It was endless. And in the beginning she believed it would be good for her. She believed she was using him to exorcise the demon, drive the snake out. That was her mistake from the beginning – to believe that at any point in her life she was in a position to make use of anything or anybody. Her fiction. I'm doing this because it suits me.

But now she *has* done something because it suited her.

'What are you going to do now?'

'The worst of it was, one night about a year ago, we had a fight. A bad fight. He hadn't hit me in two or three years, but he hit me bad that night. I had a cracked rib I think. I'm not sure because I never went to a doctor about it but it hurt whenever I took a deep breath. He never said a word about it, but I knew he'd flip if I went for help. Anyway, I was ashamed myself. But that night he told me something. He just spat it out. After all the knocking around, when I was lying in a corner of the bedroom holding on to my ribs.'

'Alice, what are you going to do now?'

'Wait. Do you remember my sister Sheila? You came to her funeral.' He nods. 'That's what he said. He said the bastard did it to her too. Before me. The same priest. I didn't believe him. I called him a liar and he laughed in my face. He said there was a family of us, all losers. He said the priest was doing it to her too. Bastard! Bastard!'

'Alice, I know you're upset, but you have to work out what to do.'

Alice points at the patio window. 'I thought you said your cat was dead?' A cat, with one foot poised against the glass is gazing quizzically at the room.

'Neighbour's cat,' Mick says. 'Here kitty kitty.' He gets down on his hands and knees and crawls to the window. 'Kitty kitty?' It occurs to Alice that he is not sober at the same moment that she realises her own drunkenness. The cat swivels away and goes down into the gloom on feet of tissue. Mick crawls back, laughing and hauling himself up into his easy chair. 'Fucking cats,' he says. 'I hate them. So fucking self-sufficient.'

Alice does not laugh. She has leaned forward, her hands folded on her knees, her head looking sideways at him. It is a curiously vulnerable position. 'What I was saying. He was sleeping with my sister Sheila when they were in college. What that fat bastard was up to, he found out about it then. He said that was probably why she went out that night. Because he was there. I remember it too. He was on his way back to the parish house when he came on the accident. If Paddy knew about her he probably knew about me too. He came after me! Not the other way round! He picked me out! He knew what I was.'

'She poisoned the cat.' Crazy bitch. He was well rid of her. Poisoned his life too, come to think of it. Every minute of dread. She was buried now and who gave a shit?

Alice shakes her head and focuses on his words with a visible effort. 'I thought it was the other way round. She poisoned herself.'

'Alice. Listen.'

'Oh Mick. You're so nice. Why didn't I marry a nice man like you instead of that bastard? We could be living happily now, the two of us, maybe a few kids.'

'Alice. Where is your one?'

'Who?'

'The one that shot him? Where did she go?'

'I don't know.'

'She might have gone to the guards.'

'No. No one went near the house.'

'I thought you said you didn't know where you were? I thought you said you drove around, that's all.'

'I drove past the house once. I just couldn't believe it happened. I thought it might have been a dream. I didn't go in though. But I could see his car. I knew if it was a dream he would be at the office.'

'Jesus Christ. Have you any idea what you're talking about?'

Suddenly she clasps her hands in front of her, a supplicant gesture, an unwise virgin before the altar. 'Oh God. Yes you're right. I have to work out what to do. I have to call the guards. I don't know where she is now. She could be gone. She might still be there. I can't go back. Paddy was lying there with blood coming out of his mouth.' It was a purple bubble that she remembered, perched on the edge of his lip, expanding slowly. And the look in Sandy's eyes. Not wild, panicked yes, but not freaked. She dropped the gun immediately. Alice remembered that it fell on to Paddy's good leg and rolled off the bed. It was strange that Paddy did not react when the gun fell on him, no reflex, no jerk of the leg, no groan. The crash of the gun landing on the floor seemed louder than the shot. She asked what she had done, and Alice said that she had killed the fucker. Oh my God, Sandy said. God had nothing to do with it, Alice said. You'd better run, Alice said. Hide. Go to Billy's, he'll hide you. What about you? Sandy said. I didn't pull the trigger, Alice said. Then Sandy went to the door and she turned at the door and said, Bitch! At that moment Alice thought Sandy would attack her. She was glad that both barrels had been discharged. He raped you remember, Alice shouted. That's your defence. He raped you. His semen is still in you. Go to a doctor. Get a sample. She heard the front door closing and her running steps on the drive. Fuck her, Alice thought. Slut. Then she turned to Paddy and looked at him. His eyes were different. There was no response in them, none of the infinitesimal adjustments that go on continuously in living things. The light and dark were all the same to him now.

Mick puts his glass down on a side table and spins

around so that he is looking straight at her. 'I'll give you an alibi.'

'What Mick?'

'I'll give you an alibi. For the time. I'll say you were here with me. Consoling me.' He winks. She puts her head on one side and her eyes fill up with tears. 'Oh Mick. You're kind.'

'I just need to get the details straight. I'm a bit confused. Tipsy.'

'It was very early. This morning.'

'Say you were sleeping with me. We've been lovers for, say a year.'

She nods. 'Lovers.'

'You'll have to do it, of course.'

Her head snaps back, eyes narrowed. 'What?'

'You know. You'll have to – to make sure. The real thing.'

'What are you talking about?'

He clasps his hands together in front of him. Alice sees that they are powerful still, the hurler's hands, the County champion. They seem to be too big for his wrists, like hammer heads on the thin spindle of the handle. 'Alice, you're not a fool,' he says. 'Neither of us is a fool. The guards are going to come looking for you and they're going to ask where you've been all day. It'll look bad.' She swallows something large. She looks at the window then at the door. Then she looks back at his hands. They are open now, a gesture to indicate guilelessness. He turns away and looks at the blank wall. 'They could easy decide to do tests. Check up the story. This DNA thing now, they say that's foolproof. We'd have to make it look right. Come upstairs with me,' he says slowly, 'for a few minutes and then we'll go to the guards.'

She stands up suddenly. 'I didn't do it,' she shouts. 'Sandy did. She shot him.'

'Fuck that!' he shouts. 'You think I'm a fool. Well I'm fucking not. I see what you're up to.' He stands too, positioning himself adroitly between her and the door. Here is the champion hurler, she thinks, a kind of dancer, always in the right place at the right time. He still has the light angular frame, the same shrug of the shoulders that she remembers from years before when he came for her sister's funeral. But it is bulbous with fat now, years of laziness and office-eating that contributed, if anything, to the impression of power. She feels a kind of weary resignation welling up. It was all for nothing.

'Calm down,' he says. 'All I'm asking is a couple of minutes of your time.'

'From time to time,' he adds. 'We'll have to keep it up until the trial is over.'

'Oh Jesus.' For an instant her eyes roam the room searching for something to strike out with. The patio door is a black rectangle, sucking light and heat outwards, nightfall as sudden and cataclysmic as a stroke. She sees the room reflected on the blackness, Mick Delany and herself, trapped in a mirror-room, a suggestion of translucence about them, as though she could step through herself and escape to another world. Then hopelessness bubbles up in her and she begins to cry, tears streaming out of open eyes, a mouth suddenly uncontrollably mobile, a child hurt and ashamed of her tears.

'I remember when you got married,' Mick is saying. He is staring at her. 'Jesus you were a beautiful bride. But you were a lot younger than him. Another few years and you could have been his child. Almost anyway.' He holds out a hand, fat, moist. 'Look,' he says. 'Stop crying. I'm your alibi. The perfect alibi.'

He catches her gently and moves her towards the door. He smiles at her and she catches the gust of whiskey on his breath. 'It'll be our secret,' he says. 'Just the two of us.' She feels his hand resting on the small of her back, a light pressure, no force. She feels herself impelled backwards towards childhood, to the dark of the hallway and realises that she belongs in this shrinking world, knows the map on the wall and all that it contains. She knows the names of the dark figures who wait in the hall to lead her inwards. She feels the fibres of her heart loosening, the resistance softening. She is a tired child, nothing more. And after all she has struggled and failed. Nothing can be expected of her. It is easier to give herself over to the other, as in childhood in times of trouble she had been able to trust her father, her mother, her sister; to give up her own will and be led by those who know best. She takes a deep breath but the air seems suffocatingly humid, sticky almost. She thinks, for a moment, that a cobweb has fallen on her face, or a piece of thin plastic, stopping the passage to her lungs. She claws at it, dragging her nails across her lips.

But there is nothing there.